Ever After High™

Kiss and Spell

Also by *Suzanne Selfors*

Ever After High™

EVER AFTER Royals!

Kiss and Spell

EVER AFTER Rebels

A SCHOOL STORY

Suzanne Selfors

ⓁⒷ

LITTLE, BROWN AND COMPANY

New York   Boston

For Elizabeth,
the nicest person
I ever met in kingdergarten

Copyright © 2015 Mattel, Inc.

Little, Brown and Company

Hachette Book Group
1290 Avenue of the Americas, New York, NY 10104
Visit us at lb-kids.com

Little, Brown and Company is a division of Hachette Book Group, Inc.
The Little, Brown name and logo are trademarks of Hachette Book Group, Inc.

The publisher is not responsible for websites (or their content)
that are not owned by the publisher.

First Edition: April 2015

Library of Congress Cataloging-in-Publication Data

Selfors, Suzanne, author.
  Kiss and spell / by Suzanne Selfors. — First edition.
    pages cm. — (Ever After High ; 2)
  Summary: Ever After High is a boarding school for the sons and daughters of fairy tale characters, and student Ginger Breadhouse, daughter of the Candy Witch, studies all the usual magic subjects—but what she is mostly interested in is making her cooking show, Spells Kitchen, a success by introducing happiness as the secret ingredient.
    ISBN 978-0-316-40131-9 (hardcover) — ISBN 978-0-316-40134-0 (ebook) — ISBN 978-0-316-40132-6 (library edition ebook) 1. Magic—Juvenile fiction. 2. High schools—Juvenile fiction. 3. Cooking—Juvenile fiction. 4. Witches—Juvenile fiction. 5. Mothers and daughters—Juvenile fiction. [1. Fairy tales—Fiction. 2. Characters in literature—Fiction. 3. Magic—Fiction. 4. Cooking—Fiction. 5. Witches—Fiction. 6. Mothers and daughters—Fiction. 7. Boarding schools—Fiction. 8. Schools—Fiction.] I. Title.
  PZ7.S456922Ki 2015
  [Fic]—dc23   2014036678

10 9 8 7 6 5 4 3 2 1

RRD-C

Printed in the United States of America

Contents

Dear reader,

Look for this 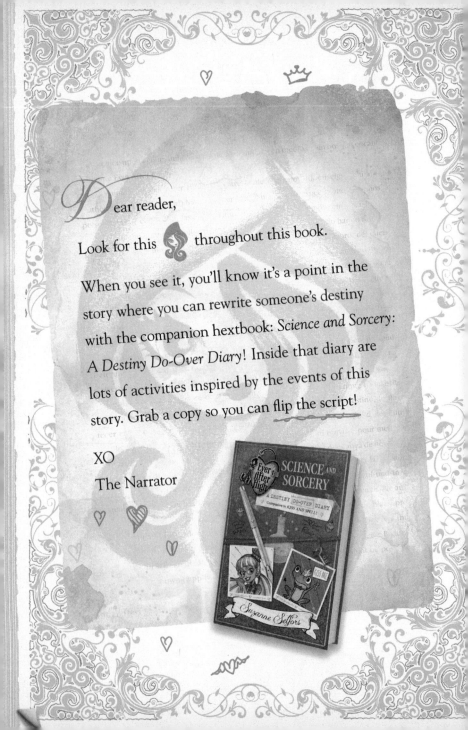 throughout this book.

When you see it, you'll know it's a point in the story where you can rewrite someone's destiny with the companion hextbook: *Science and Sorcery: A Destiny Do-Over Diary*! Inside that diary are lots of activities inspired by the events of this story. Grab a copy so you can flip the script!

XO
The Narrator

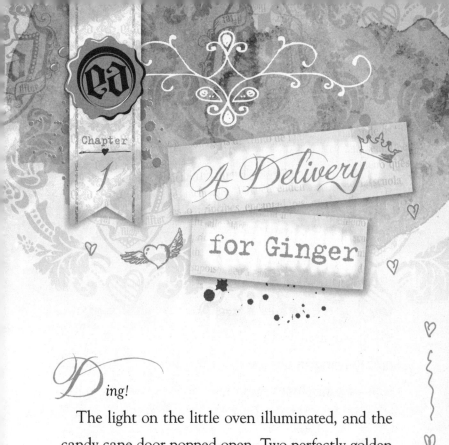

A Delivery for Ginger

*D*ing!

The light on the little oven illuminated, and the candy cane door popped open. Two perfectly golden muffins sat inside.

"Yum!" Melody Piper threw back her quilt and scrambled out of bed.

"Be careful. They're hot," Ginger Breadhouse warned. She'd been baking muffins since she was a child, so she knew they needed at least a minute to cool.

But Melody didn't care. She loved Ginger's treats so much she was willing to risk a burnt finger or tongue. She slid one of the muffins onto a plate and began to carefully peel back the foil. "I have to admit, when I met you on the first day of school, I thought it was really weird that you'd brought your toy oven. But now I think it's fableous!"

Ginger smiled, remembering how she'd lugged her trunk up the dormitory stairs with the Princess-Bake Oven strapped to the top. Perhaps it had seemed a bit odd to bring an old toy to school, but it was a *beloved* toy—a reminder of sweet moments in her happy and carefree youth. She'd set it on her dormitory desk next to her cookbook collection, and whenever she looked at it, she remembered those days as a little girl when she'd played alone in her room, making her very first treats. Though she'd long outgrown the toy oven, it was still fun to use, now and then.

"If I'd had one of these when I was little, I would have cooked all the time," Melody said. "This muffin is delicious. What's the secret ingredient? Magic?"

"A chef never gives away her secrets," Ginger said with a twinkle in her eye. The truth was, it wasn't magic. It was simply a tiny chandelier that got hot enough to turn batter into cake. But even if the muffins had been baked by a cooking charm or a sweet spell, no one would have raised an eyebrow. Magic was everywhere at Ever After High, a boarding school for the sons and daughters of fairytale characters. Ginger was the daughter of the Candy Witch, and Melody was the daughter of the Pied Piper. Though the two girls had different interests— Melody wanted to be a DJ, while Ginger wanted to be a professional pastry chef—they got along quite well as roommates. Each respected the other's drive and passion.

"I gotta run," Ginger said, quickly pulling her long pink hair into ponytails. "You can have the other muffin."

"Where are you going?" Melody asked, her mouth full.

"To the mail room. It's delivery day," Ginger

reminded her. "See ya later." She waved good-bye to Melody, then to her pet fish, Jelly. He swam to the top of his tank, poked his yellow head above the water, and smiled at her. He might have been made of candy, but he still acted like a real fish.

Bye, Jelly said with a smack of his tail.

"Bye," Melody called as Ginger hurried out the door.

The mail room was all the way across campus, which meant Ginger had to descend a dozen staircases, dart down seven hallways, weave around three fountains, cross two bridges, and duck beneath a sagging arch to get there. Many students were heading to breakfast in the Castleteria. "Hey, Ginger, I really loved those massive macaroons," called Raven Queen, daughter of the universally feared Evil Queen.

"Can't wait to see what you whip up next," said Cedar Wood, daughter of Pinocchio, the most famous puppet in all the kingdoms.

Ginger smiled proudly. To be appreciated for

her baking was a dream come true. The Castle-teria's breakfast offerings of runny pigeon eggs and scorched porridge were hard to swallow, so Ginger tried to bring treats as often as possible. "Thanks!" She continued her hurried pace, down a narrow stone staircase and between a pair of griffin statues. Finally, a bit out of breath but giddy with expectation, she reached her destination.

By fairytale standards, the mail room at Ever After High wasn't worth a second glance. It paled in comparison with the grand design of the school library, where bookshelves were nestled between gigantic trees and enchanting tomes of yesteryear waited to be discovered. It couldn't compete with the foreboding cauldron room, where briny brews toiled and bubbled and where villainous plans were concocted. And it was totally boring compared with the Charmitorium, where chandelier light danced upon a gilded stage and princesses sat in plush box seats.

The dusty, old mail room didn't stand out in

any way—just a neglected space with some walls, a floor, a ceiling, and a counter. And because the current students received messages from home on their MirrorPhones, there were no stacks of envelopes or scrolls waiting to be picked up, as there had been in generations past. However, a few packages still arrived on the 9:00 AM delivery coach.

"Hello?" Ginger called. She tapped the little bell. "Hello? Is there a delivery for me?"

A snort sounded. The lady who worked the counter peeked out of the back room. Her face was as ugly as a troll's, on account of her being a troll. "Whadda ya want?" She held an issue of *Troll Times* magazine. The lead article: "The Latest Hairstyles for Your Feet."

"May I please have my package?"

"What's yer name?"

"Ginger Breadhouse."

The troll lady scratched under her armpit. "Ginger who?"

"Breadhouse. Ginger *Breadhouse*." Ginger frowned.

The troll lady should have known her name by now. Ginger came to the mail room once a week for her special deliveries.

"Lemme check." Sounds of searching rose from the back room—shuffling footsteps, boxes being moved about, and grunting. Lots and lots of grunting.

Ginger tapped her fingers on the counter. "It's from the Fairytale Food Emporium," she explained. "It's a box of special baking chocolate from Candy Mountain. It comes right off the mountainside. It's for—"

"Yeah, yeah, hold yer horses." More grunting. Then the troll lady shuffled out of the back room and set a small box on the counter. "Sign here." She pointed a hairy finger at the delivery receipt.

Ginger penned her swirly signature, looping the *g* and turning the *o* into a smiley face. She wrote as if decorating a cake, and that was how she dressed, too.

Upon first glance, one might find Ginger a bit, well, *overstated*. But her colorful wardrobe choices weren't made because she wanted attention. She'd spent most of her life trying to blend in and hide her true identity. (More on that later.) But her passion for baking scrumptious treats grew with each year, and it began to influence everything about her, including her appearance.

Ginger's skirt and jacket were accented with gumdrop buttons and swirls that looked as if they'd come from the tip of an icing dispenser. Even her shoes seemed to have been dipped in frosting. A bright candy-confection necklace and a cupcake-shaped hat completed the sweet statement. With her pink hair and pink glasses, Ginger was a colorful sight. *Everything looks better with a little decoration*, she believed. *Or a cherry on top.* Which was why she stared at the troll lady's drab brown dress and rope belt. If only she'd add a ribbon of blue along the hem or a sprinkle of yellow on the collar.

"Chocolate, ya say?" The troll lady scratched her hairy chin. "You shouldn't be eating chocolate. It'll give ya pimples."

Ginger adjusted her glasses. The troll lady appeared

to be an expert on that particular subject, seeing that a fair number of pustules were sprouting on her nose. "Actually, I'm using the chocolate to make glaze for my spelly doughnuts," Ginger told her. "On my cooking MirrorCast, *Spells Kitchen*." She beamed proudly. But the troll lady showed no signs of recognition. "You haven't heard of my show? I teach people how to bake yummy things."

"I don't watch shows that teach ya stuff. I like *Housewives of Troll County*." She picked a bit of food from her single tooth. "Those gals really know how to throw a punch." She ate the bit of food. "You seen that new show, *Daring's Day*? That one's real good. You don't learn nothin'."

Ginger didn't admit that she *had* spent a whole hour yesterday watching *Daring's Day*, a reality MirrorCast that focused on Ever After High's most popular prince, Daring Charming. Nor did she admit that she was minty green with jealousy because he had more views for a single episode than all of her episodes combined. Students liked to eat her treats, but they didn't seem interested in learning how to make them. "Thanks for the package," she said. Then she tucked the box under her arm and headed outside.

The quad was busy this morning as students gathered to chat. With her heels clicking along the cobblestones, Ginger shook away the feelings of doubt. So what if she didn't have as many views or crownloads as Daring Charming? Once she'd graduated from Ever After High, she'd open her own chain of bakeries. She'd publish cookbooks and create an entire line of gourmet treats under her label, Ginger's Goodies. By sharing her talents on a larger scale, she'd help make the world a happier place. For Ginger Breadhouse believed, with every ounce, gram, and sprinkle of her soul, that good food was one of the secret ingredients to happiness. Whether in times of celebration or sadness, beautifully prepared goodies had the power to bring people together.

She smiled as her thoughts drifted toward the destiny she wanted with all her heart.

"Hey, watch it!" someone grumbled.

"Sorry," Ginger said. She'd been so caught up in her daydreams she'd bumped right into a group of girls who were standing in the center of the quad, holding their hocus lattes. "What's going on?"

"Daring," one of them said, then pointed to an enormous mirror that hung from one of the school's grand trees. As Ginger peered over their shoulders, the title DARING'S DAY flashed on the mirror screen. The girls squealed as the prince's face appeared. He was brushing his thick blond hair.

"He's soooo dreamy," one of the girls said.

"This is the best show ever after," another girl chirped. She wore a shirt that read: TEAM DARING.

Daring smiled into the camera, nearly blinding the viewers with his dazzlingly white teeth. Then he set the brush aside and spritzed cologne on his neck. The camera closed in on the bottle. Its label read: BE DARING. "Available in eight-ounce and one-gallon jugs at the Ever After High Bookstore," Daring told his viewers.

Like bees seeking pollen, the groupies swarmed toward the bookstore. They all tried to cram into the doorway at the same time. "Me first!" "Out of my way!" "I'm buying three jugs!"

Product placement, Ginger thought. *How very clever.* She didn't have any product placement on her show. But she wasn't famous like Daring Charming.

"Hi, Ginger." Ashlynn Ella, the daughter of Cinderella, waved as she passed by.

"Hi, Ginger." Holly O'Hair, daughter of Rapunzel, also waved.

"Hi," Ginger called. She appreciated the kindness that many of the students offered her.

But that hadn't always been the case. Although most students loved her sweets and thought she was a nice person, others were suspicious of Ginger, on account of her fairytale destiny.

Unlike Ashlynn and Holly, Ginger Breadhouse was not the daughter of a popular princess. She was the daughter of a witch.

The Candy Witch.

Snacky

Time

itches come in all shapes and sizes. Some spend their lives in isolation. Some ride brooms and terrorize villagers. Some do magic tricks at birthday parties.

And some are nice, while others are wicked.

Ginger's mother was of the latter variety. She was the Candy Witch, the very woman rumored to have lured Hansel and Gretel into her gingerbread house, locked Hansel in a cage, then tried to fatten him up so she could roast him for dinner.

But that was one big lie. The truth was that Hansel and Gretel were nasty little children who didn't have an ounce of manners between them. They'd been out in the Dark Forest one day, stomping on things and ignoring NO TRESPASSING signs, when they saw a house covered in candy. So, without asking permission or waiting to be invited, they started to eat the house. Then, wanting more candy, they climbed through a window and started eating the interior. When the Candy Witch caught them, she was very upset. "How would you like it if I ate your house?"

"But our house is made of bricks," Hansel said, a candy cane drawer handle sticking out of his mouth.

"*Ja,* und made of mortar," Gretel added between bites of a licorice rope curtain.

The Candy Witch frowned. "That is *not* the point. The point is, dearies, my house belongs to me, not you. And it is very rude to eat something that belongs to someone else."

"Ve don't care," Hansel and Gretel said.

So the Candy Witch called their parents, and when faced with a month of being grounded, Hansel and Gretel lied. "Ve ate zee candy because zee vicked vitch forced us!" Gretel said, candy corn stuck to her teeth.

"Und then she tried to cook us in de stew pot," Hansel added, wiping chocolate from his round cheeks.

"*Ja.* She vants to eat us vith dumplings."

The horrid parents believed their horrid children. They told everyone they knew that Hansel and Gretel had outsmarted the wicked witch, barely escaping with their lives. The fable quickly spread, from castle turret to sod hut. And because no one ever believes a witch, Hansel and Gretel's version of the story was written into the Storybook of Legends. Thus, the Candy Witch's reputation as a child-eating monster stuck to her like gooey caramel.

But even though she had no interest in consuming

children, the Candy Witch still had a dark side. She was an expert at making evil potions. And she used them.

The reason why she made evil potions was simple— she'd been born into a long line of wicked witches. And when one is wicked, one doesn't make *nice* potions. Her mother and grandmother taught her the witchy ways. Huddling over a steaming cauldron, brewing something vile, was what the women in her family did. She accepted her legacy with pride. Over the years, she had created a vast collection of potions. Some grew fur on bare skin. Some made ears double in size. Others stole voices. She always needed test subjects and learned, early on, that it was much easier to get a victim to eat an evil potion if it was hidden in a delicious treat. Who could resist the allure of a cupcake with buttercream frosting? Or a gingerbread boy with gumdrop buttons? It didn't take long for the local villagers to realize that the sweet treats from the Candy Witch's kitchen were responsible for the unwanted tails and horns on their children. But she continued her quest, creating unpleasant potions, testing them, and publishing the results in academic and professional witch journals.

Childhood was, therefore, quite difficult for Ginger. When your parent has a thriving career as a wicked witch, and a reputation as a child-eater, you're destined to have trouble making friends. No parents allowed their children to visit the Candy Witch's house, so Ginger was quite lonely. "Don't go near that place. The witch who lives there will eat you up!" the neighbors warned.

"My mom doesn't eat kids!" Ginger shouted out the gumdrop-lined window. "That's a mean thing to say!" But no one seemed to believe her.

And thus, Ginger's days passed, friendless.

But then came a wonderful new opportunity called kingdergarten.

Because the local spellementary school didn't want anything to do with the Candy Witch—or her child—it was arranged for Ginger to be schooled in a different fairytale district. A horseless carriage picked her up before sunrise. On that first day, even though the journey was long, she was too excited to nap. The days at home, with nothing to do but watch her mother brew poisoned potions, had become as monotonous as waiting for water to boil. She'd felt like Rapunzel, locked in a tower, only Ginger hadn't been waiting for a prince—she'd been waiting to make friends.

When she stepped out of the carriage at Aesop's Spellementary School, no one ran away in terror. When she walked into the kingdergarten classroom, no one shrieked in fear. Having no idea about Ginger's wicked heritage, the teacher welcomed her. On that first day, Ginger played leapfrog, made a macaroni crown, and learned the names of every student. She'd never felt happier. As days grew into weeks, she didn't mind the long carriage journey to and from school, because the hours there became the best hours of her life.

Until it was her turn for snack time.

Each day after recess, a different parent brought

snacks to the kingdergarten classroom. All sorts of lovely things were delivered, like Three Blind Mice cheese wedges, beanstalk butter sandwiches, and iced royal crumpets. The teacher, Sister Goose, would hand out the snacks, and the kingdergartners would munch happily.

But unbeknownst to Ginger, her mother had signed up for snack duty as well.

When the Candy Witch walked into the classroom, the students gasped. Because they lived in a fairytale kingdom, they were used to seeing all sorts of beings, like fairies, trolls, and such. So they knew a witch when they came face-to-face with one. The Candy Witch, with her black military boots, ragged black dress, and green matted hair, could have been the poster woman for wicked witches. In fact, she had once been on the cover of *Wicked Witch Monthly*. The editors hadn't even needed to Photoshop a wart onto her chin, because she already had one. She did, however, like to accessorize with candy. A gummy slug necklace was her favorite piece of jewelry.

"Hello, my little sweetlings," she said in her shrill voice. "Who would like a little snackypoo?"

Sister Goose stepped protectively in front of her students. "And who might you be?"

"I'm the Candy…" She paused, then cackled. "I'm Ms. Breadhouse, Ginger's mother. Today is my day for snack duty."

Everyone turned and looked at Ginger. She felt her cheeks go red.

The Candy Witch held a tray of yellow cookies, decorated like perfect smiley faces. "Eat your treats, my little lovelies." She grinned, exposing her blackened teeth. Then she stomped around the room, placing a cookie on each student's desk.

"Don't eat those!" Sister Goose exclaimed. "This woman is a witch, and a wicked one at that. I can tell just by looking at her." She peered over the top of her glasses. "In fact, I know exactly who she is. She's the Candy Witch, and she came here to eat us all."

Ginger wanted to crawl under her desk and hide

from the embarrassment. Everyone was staring at her.

"Eat you? Why would I do that? I am curious, though, dear, if you'd taste better boiled or fried." When the teacher gasped, the Candy Witch cackled. "I'm kidding. I'm kidding. It's a witchy joke, nothing more."

"If you didn't come here to eat us, then you came here to poison us with one of your potions," Sister Goose said. "Everyone knows you make *evil* potions."

The Candy Witch shrugged. "Okay, I admit it. I added a bit of shrinking potion. So sue me. It's all in good fun." She held out a smiley cookie. "Give it a try."

"You are forbidden to bring snacks to our class again!" Sister Goose grabbed a wastebasket and threw each cookie away. Then she crossed MS. BREADHOUSE off the snack-duty list.

"I'm sensing you're not fond of sweets," the Candy Witch said drily.

After that incident, none of the other kids hung

out with Ginger. Invitations to birthday parties and requests for playdates stopped. She sat alone at recess and lunch. The carriage ride to and from school became unbearably long. "I hate school," she told her mother. "I don't want to go anymore."

"I sense this is my fault," her mother said while mashing tarantula guts.

Because Ginger was only six years old, she was too young to understand the depth of the situation. All she knew, at that moment, was that she felt very bad because she'd worked hard to make friends, and now she didn't have any. "Why can't you be like the other parents?" Ginger asked, her eyes filling with tears.

"I'll never be like other parents, sweetie. One day you'll appreciate me for who I am."

"But it's so unfair!" She ran upstairs to her bedroom and slammed the door.

A long while passed with Ginger facedown on her bed, crying into her Cinderella pillow. As she rolled over to blow her nose, a knock sounded. Her mother's voice came from the other side of the door.

"Gingerpoo?" she called. "If I make a batch of your favorite spelly doughnuts, will you come out of your room?"

"No evil potions inside?"

"No evil potions. Just sugar and love."

Ginger threw the door open and hugged her mom.

Kissing

Booth

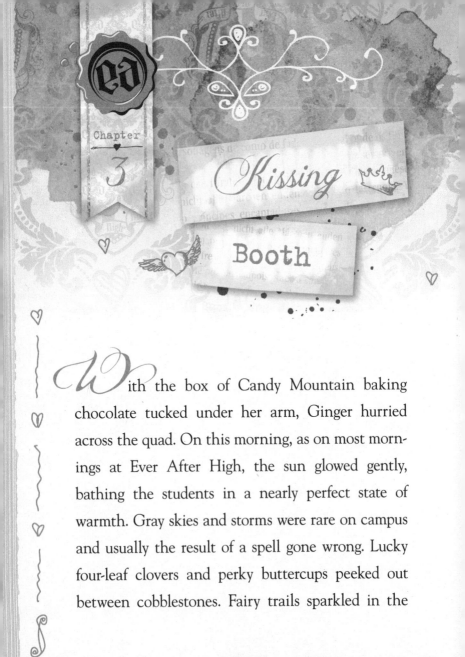

With the box of Candy Mountain baking chocolate tucked under her arm, Ginger hurried across the quad. On this morning, as on most mornings at Ever After High, the sun glowed gently, bathing the students in a nearly perfect state of warmth. Gray skies and storms were rare on campus and usually the result of a spell gone wrong. Lucky four-leaf clovers and perky buttercups peeked out between cobblestones. Fairy trails sparkled in the air, and a scent drifted from an open Castleteria window, tickling Ginger's nose. *Stone soup*, she thought. Like most good cooks, Ginger possessed a heightened sense of taste and smell. She detected a dash of pickled pepper in the soup, nothing more. It was a boring recipe, but Hagatha, the school's cook, was not known for her inventive menus. If Ginger had been tasked with making the stone soup, she would have added a hint of possibility—a delightful flavor enhancer.

As she imagined what kind of dessert she might serve after the soup, Ginger stopped in her tracks. Was she seeing what she thought she was seeing? She slid her pink glasses up the bridge of her nose and blinked hard.

Hopper Croakington II, son of the Frog Prince, stood directly across the quad. And around his neck hung a sign that read: KISS ME.

What in Ever After? Ginger wondered. Normally, she wouldn't be interested in a boy wearing a KISS

ME sign. But she'd been secretly crushing on Hopper since the first day of school. Who could resist those adorable freckles and big green eyes? Or that carefree, tousled chestnut hair? But it wasn't just his good looks that attracted Ginger. She liked his unique qualities. First, he possessed his own sense of style, preferring embroidered jackets, tailored vests, khaki shorts, and loafers. Some might call it a look of privilege, worn by a boy who had lived a life of entitlement, but Ginger saw it as quirky. She admired quirky. And second, though Hopper tended to hang out with boys like Sparrow Hood (son of Robin Hood) and Daring Charming, he also had a few friends on the more geeky side of the fence, like the Tech Club guys. It was part of Hopper's dual nature—like a cookie that's ornately frosted on one side and wholesomely plain on the other.

But what was he doing now?

Hopper stood inside a booth, leaning on a counter. A big jar sat next to him. Above his head, a banner read:

TECH CLUB KISSING BOOTH
~~5 DOLLARS~~ PER KISS
~~3 Dollars~~ 1 Dollar

The jar was empty.

Then Ginger understood what was going on. School clubs and teams often set up fund-raising tables and booths in the quad. Last week the cheer-hexers held a bake sale. They'd relied on Ginger to provide most of the treats, which she'd been happy to do. After that, the Applebatics team held a raffle. The winning ticket-holder won an apple pie, baked by Ginger, of course. Today it appeared to be the Tech Club's turn. Ginger knew most of the members of the Tech Club because they helped record her MirrorCast show. Hopper was the newest member, having just joined last week in order to get some hextra credit.

"Don't be shy, kiss a tech guy." The Tech Club president, Humphrey Dumpty, son of the accident-prone

Humpty Dumpty, was trying to catch the attention of a few passing students. He stood outside the booth, his glasses bobbing as he rapped, "*Only a buck, try your luck.*" No one seemed to be paying attention. He put his hands on his hips and frowned. "Come on, people. We need money to update our equipment."

Ginger stared at the booth. She could barely contain her smile. This was the most spelltacular thing that had happened since she'd gotten that special delivery of singing sprinkles last month. She could never work up the courage to tell Hopper how she felt. But there he stood with a big invitation hanging from his neck. Was this her chance to sneak a little kiss, without having to admit her true feelings?

"Hey, Hopper," a voice called.

Just as Hopper looked up, Ginger darted behind a tree. Had he seen her? Her heart began to pound. She didn't want to be caught staring. On the other hand, wasn't it worse to be caught hiding? Why did she get so brainswished around him? She could cook a seventeen-course meal without flinching, but one

look from Hopper and her brain got as soft as plum pudding. Cautiously, she peered out from behind the tree's trunk.

Sparrow Hood strolled up to the booth, his guitar slung over his shoulder. "Are you working, dude?"

"Yeah," Hopper told him. "I'm helping Humphrey raise money."

"Money?" Sparrow sang the word. The studs on his leather jacket glinted in the sunlight. "I love money, but why work for it? Just ask your family for some dough, bro."

Humphrey stopped rapping. "We don't need our parents," he explained to Sparrow. "We're going to earn the money on our own."

"Earn the money?" Sparrow struck a chord on his guitar. *"What a concept,"* he sang. A nearby bird squawked in protest. "How much have you made?"

"Nothing," Humphrey said with a big sigh. "I'm beginning to suspect that no one wants to kiss us."

"Speak for yourself," Hopper said, his voice full of bravado. "Obviously, the only reason girls aren't

stopping to kiss *me* is because they're all too busy."
He smoothed one of his embroidered sleeves, then
the other. "I mean, look around. No one's out here."
At that very moment, some of the girls from the
cheerhexing squad passed by.

"Hello, ladies," Hopper said, puckering his lips.
"No need to wince! Why not kiss a prince?"

None of the girls stopped.

Sparrow strummed a few chords, then sang,
"Awkward."

Poor Hopper. No one seemed interested in kissing him. And Sparrow was being a big tease. Ginger
reached into her jacket's inner pocket and pulled
out a five-dollar bill. At the current rate, that would
buy five kisses. She frowned. Who was she kidding?
She didn't have the courage to buy even a single
kiss. But maybe, if she hurried past, she could sneak
her money into the jar. Then Hopper wouldn't feel
totally rejected. She peered around the trunk.

Sparrow scratched his chin. "Well, I wish you
dudes the best of luck, but I've got band practice with

the Merry Men. Catch ya later." After a long guitar riff, he strolled away.

"I'm going, too," Hopper told Humphrey.

"Don't go yet," Humphrey pleaded. He adjusted his bow tie. "Just a few more minutes. I'm sure some girls will stop. Look, here comes Briar."

"*Briar?*" Hopper's voice cracked when he said her name. Briar Beauty, daughter of Sleeping Beauty, was one of the most popular princesses at Ever After High. And everyone knew that Hopper was madly crushing on her.

Humphrey and Hopper stared, openmouthed, as Briar and her friend Apple White approached. Apple was the daughter of Snow White. Both girls were princesses with Happily Ever After destinies. They were close friends and had become even closer because of the recent uprising of the Rebels—Ever After High students who didn't want to embrace their prewritten destinies. Ginger never called herself a Rebel, but she certainly wanted to choose her own path.

Humphrey started rapping again, bouncing around in an odd, wobbly way on his skinny legs. Ginger thought he should be more careful, given that his destiny was to fall and break into pieces. *"Why not try your luck and pucker up?"*

Hopper leaned on the booth's counter and wagged his eyebrows. "Whassup, ladies?" He was trying to act smooth, but whenever he got around Briar, Hopper was about as smooth as an ogremeal cookie. "People call me Hopper, but you can call me tonight." He made a smooching sound and pointed to his cheek.

Briar and Apple stopped walking. Briar pushed her crownglasses onto her forehead. "Let me get this straight. You want *us* to pay *you*?" She smiled. "For a kiss?" Apple giggled. "Have you guys flipped your crowns?"

"I'd like to flip *your* crown," Hopper said, staring at Briar.

Briar put her hands on her hips. "What does that mean, exactly?"

"Uh…" Hopper paused.

And then something terrible happened. Ginger saw it coming a mile away. Often when Hopper tried to talk to Briar, he ended up blushing. And whenever he blushed, he...

Poof!

...turned into a frog.

The *poof* was accompanied by a little cloud. Hopper the boy disappeared, and Hopper the frog materialized. For a moment, he hung in midair as if suspended by invisible thread, his little green legs kicking madly. Then Hopper and the KISS ME sign landed on the counter. After adjusting his tiny gold crown, he rose onto his hind legs and said, in a deep voice, "Has fortune smiled upon me? Do I glimpse the fair Briar waiting in line to plant a delicate kiss upon my cheek? If so, I shall never wash that cheek again."

This was yet another example of Hopper's dual nature—in frog form he was poetic and smooth, but in human form he came across as awkward and smarmy. He tried so hard but managed to say the wrong thing time and time again. His pickup lines were the worst.

"Very funny, but no thanks." Briar slid her crown-glasses back onto her nose, then yawned super wide. It was in her DNA to fall asleep anytime, anywhere, so she tended to yawn a lot.

Apple, who tried to be nice to everyone, took some money from her book bag. "I'm happy to donate to the cause," she said, stuffing the bills into the jar. "But I'm saving all my kisses for my future Prince Charming." Then she and Briar walked away.

As they passed by the tree, Ginger overhead Briar whisper, "Hopper always says the weirdest stuff." Then she yawned again.

"He's just trying to impress you," Apple said sweetly. Then they disappeared around a hedge that had been trimmed into the letters *EAH*.

Hopper the frog crossed his little green arms. "It would appear that my attempts to entice the gentler gender hath been in vain." Then *poof*, the spell wore off and he was back in boy form. The transformation never seemed to last very long. His curse, to be a frog forever until a princess kissed him, was not supposed to happen until he was an adult.

Ginger leaned away from the tree so she could get a better look at Hopper's face. His downcast eyes and slumped shoulders told her that her suspicions were true: While he tried to play it cool on the outside, on the inside he was as vulnerable to rejection as anyone else. "Every time I try to talk to Briar, I turn into a frog," Hopper complained. "It drives me crazy. Girls don't like frogs. They think they're slimy."

I don't mind frogs, Ginger wanted to say.

Humphrey patted Hopper's shoulder. "Let's keep trying. I'm sure that—"

"Why bother?" Hopper suddenly straightened and cleared his throat. "It's their loss," he said, puffing out his chest. "They don't know what they're missing." Then, after adjusting his gold crown, he sauntered away. Even though he'd used the word *they*, Ginger knew he was talking about one girl—Briar.

"Don't feel bad," Humphrey said, hurrying after him. "They don't want to kiss me, either!"

Poor Hopper, Ginger thought. She knew how deeply rejection stung. But she also knew that not everything was as it appeared. A pickled lemon pie might be unbearably sour, but after a few bites, it yields other complex flavors.

She glanced at her MirrorPhone. *Uh-oh.* It was getting late and she still needed to set up before her MirrorCast show. As she left the quad, she wished there was some way she could help Hopper feel better.

Cooking

Lessons

fter the snack disaster, Ginger was not welcome at Aesop's Spellementary School, so she finished her kingdergarten year at home, with her mother. The Candy Witch was a pretty-smart cookie who was able to cover most subjects, but her favorite way to teach was in the kitchen.

It wasn't an ordinary kitchen. One side was dedicated to the art of creating evil recipes. The other side was set up for making yummy, enticing treats. On some days, Ginger sat on a stool while her

mother taught her how to brew potions that would make people burp fire and hiccup steam. Other days, she'd sit on the opposite stool and learn how to mix buttercream frosting and melt chocolate. "The goodies must be pretty so no one suspects that the recipe is evil," her mother said.

Ginger didn't like the evil-recipe days. The foulest ingredients were required—like rotten toadstools, snail slime, and worm casings. If it grew in a swamp or crawled along the moist forest floor, it usually ended up in the pantry. She accompanied her mother on field trips to collect slugs and grubs. But Ginger refused to cut up spider legs or dice wiggling worms. And she hated the cauldron, with its weird, briny scent and thick, bubbling brews. "How will you grow up to be a witch if you don't learn how to toil over a cauldron?" her mother asked worriedly.

"I'm not going to be a witch," Ginger replied. Even though she was very young, she already knew this in her heart.

"But, lovey-dovey, your destiny is already written.

You must follow your story. If you don't..." She shuddered. "I dread to think what might happen."

Ginger folded her arms and gave her mother a look of determination. "I'll figure it out."

Her mother cackled. "I suspect you will."

While Ginger didn't like the evil-recipe days, she certainly loved the treat-making days. She liked rolling dough and cutting it into perfect shapes. She liked grating chocolate into curlicues and pouring syrups into lollipop molds. But because her mother insisted on teaching the other, icky stuff, the fun lessons didn't happen enough for Ginger. She wanted to learn more about baking treats. So, one night, after the Candy Witch had gone to sleep, Ginger crept downstairs. Though she'd never cooked on her own before, she was determined to make something. She poked through the pantry, searching between bundles of dried roots, bags of swamp weeds, and jars of pickled worms. She found a couple of hen eggs, a bag of flour, some butter, and some goat milk. Then she found a recipe in a nonpoisonous cookbook and made herself a thronecake. The first few attempts didn't go well. The first was burnt on the bottom. The second was raw in the middle. But she tried and tried and finally got the hang of it, ending up with a short stack, perfectly golden and crisp at the edges. Dawn was rising, so she took her plate outside and sat on the front stoop.

"Whatcha got there?" the milk boy asked as he set two bottles of goat milk on the step. He was apparently new to the job, because he didn't seem to realize that the house belonged to the Candy Witch.

"Thronecakes," Ginger said. And she gave him one.

He gobbled it up. "That's the best thronecake I've ever had. Who made it?"

"I did," Ginger said proudly.

The milk boy parked his donkey cart, then sat next to Ginger. "Can I have another?"

"Sure." And that was the day Ginger learned a very important lesson. She could make new friends by cooking delicious treats.

Spells

Kitchen

inger's MirrorCast show, *Spells Kitchen*, was
shot inside the Cooking Class-ic classroom. The
show's format was simple—Ginger shared a new
recipe and demonstrated how to make it. Students
and teachers could watch "live" if they wanted, or
they could crownload the show and watch it at their
convenience. Ginger had hoped that the live format
would entice people to watch. Cooking live, without editing, was risky. Would she make a mistake?
Would the partridge yolks curdle? Would the soufflé

collapse? That kind of tension made for more exciting viewing.

Ginger had high hopes for her show. A well-rated school MirrorCast might lead to a national show. Which might lead to cookbooks and a chain of bakeries and candy stores, and then she could share her goodies with all the kingdoms. That was the future she wanted. The destiny she'd planned.

As usual, Ginger was the first to arrive. After turning on the lights, she set the box of Candy Mountain baking chocolate aside. Then she measured various ingredients into little containers and set them on the counter. She collected the bowls, pans, and utensils. She made sure that everything was clean and that the stove was gleaming. Unlike hosts of other cooking shows, Ginger didn't cook ahead of time and leave a final product sitting in the oven ready to eat. There was no need, because the classroom's oven was fueled by dragon fire, which meant it cooked everything extra quickly. The flame was treated with a magical spell, so it never extinguished.

After everything was ready, Humphrey Dumpty, Dexter Charming (Daring's brother), and two other students shuffled in, carrying bags of equipment. As members of the Tech Club, they worked the cameras, the microphones, and the lighting.

"Where's Hopper?" Dexter asked. "I thought he was going to earn hextra credit by helping us." Ginger listened intently as she tied a pink apron around her waist.

"He's got a stomachache or something," Humphrey said. He unzipped a bag and set a camera on a tripod. "He went back to his room. I'm guessing it was Hagatha's stone soup."

Ginger sighed. She'd been looking forward to having Hopper on the crew today. It would have been nice to look out and see his cute face.

If Hopper did have a stomachache, Ginger suspected it was from hurt feelings, though Hagatha's cooking had been known to cause digestion issues.

"Don't start without me!" a voice announced. Blondie Lockes, daughter of Goldilocks, burst into the room, her ever-present MirrorPad in hand. "Am I late? I was busy chasing a fable. Of course, I can't tell you what it is. You'll have to watch my show." She bounded between the cameras, her golden curls bouncing.

Like Ginger and Daring, Blondie also had a MirrorCast show. It was called *Just Right*, and it was the up-to-the-minute source for anything juicy at Ever After High. Secret romances, Royal dramas, or Rebel plans—Blondie uncovered whatever was trying to stay hidden. When not in class, she could be found snooping around the halls, eavesdropping, and peering through windows—whatever it took to get the latest scoop. And even if the information she collected was rumor, she considered herself a serious journalist.

"You're not late," Ginger said as she adjusted her cupcake chef's hat. "I'm glad you're here." Ginger could always trust Blondie to be honest about her cooking. She'd invited her onto the set because she needed Blondie's help.

"Five minutes to airtime," Humphrey called. As he plugged in a cord, it got tangled around his skinny legs. Everyone gasped as he face-planted onto the floor. Then the room went silent. Humphrey rolled over and felt his head. "I'm okay. Nothing cracked. No need to call the king's horses or the king's men." Everyone sighed with relief.

"I'm so glad you could help me today," Ginger said as she handed a creamy yellow apron to Blondie. "The recipe is a bit complicated." That wasn't exactly true. Ginger could handle the recipe just fine by herself. But she hoped that having Blondie as a guest would entice more students to watch. Blondie was well known around campus, since her show was one of the most watched.

"Well, I'm not a very good cook, but I can tell if something is too hot or too cold," Blondie said with a smile. "What's that?" She pointed to a stained recipe card.

"It's my mom's recipe for spelly doughnuts."

"Your *mom's* recipe?" Blondie grabbed the card

and read it. Then she leaned close to Ginger, lowering her voice to a whisper. "Are you serious? It says here these doughnuts turn whoever eats them into pink pigs."

"Don't worry," Ginger whispered back. She pointed to the card. "Look, I crossed out the part about the pink poison. No one will turn into a pig. I promise."

"Phew," Blondie said. "That's a relief."

It hurt Ginger's feelings that one of her friends could think she'd be capable of poisoning the spelly doughnuts. Even though Ginger *had* never and *would* never make one of her mother's evil recipes, people assumed she'd follow in her mother's wicked bootsteps. But Ginger wasn't the only student at Ever After High who didn't want to follow a predestined path of villainy.

"One minute," Humphrey warned.

"What do I do?" Blondie asked.

"Just follow my lead," Ginger told her friend. She checked to make sure everything was in order. Then she flipped her ponytails behind her shoulders, smoothed her apron, and looked directly into Camera 1.

Humphrey raised his hand. "Lights! Camera! Action!"

Theme song music filled the classroom. Ginger blinked for a moment, her eyes adjusting to the spotlight. As she began to speak, the music faded.

"Welcome to *Spells Kitchen*, where good food is the secret ingredient to happiness. My name's Ginger Breadhouse, and today my friend Blondie Lockes is going to help me make a fableous batch of spelly doughnuts." Blondie waved.

The show progressed without a hitch. The two girls mixed the ingredients to form dough, then plopped small balls of it into the deep fryer. They melted the baking chocolate over a gentle dragon flame. "The key to these doughnuts is, of course, the jam," Ginger explained. "You can choose any flavor jam you like, but I'm using fairyberry because it's most people's favorite."

After filling each doughnut with jam, Ginger

dipped them into the chocolate sauce. "Hex this out." She set one on a glass plate and offered it to Blondie.

"Are you sure I'm not going to turn into a pig?" Blondie whispered.

"I promise." Ginger looked out at the crew. Dexter and Humphrey were licking their lips. Too bad Hopper wasn't on the ladder, tending to the spotlight. Ginger would have made a spelly doughnut just for him. Eating something delicious might have made him feel better about the whole kissing-booth fiasco. At the very least, it would have sugarcoated his disappointment.

Hesitantly, Blondie held the doughnut to her lips and took the tiniest of bites. "Yum, it's good," she said. Then she put a hand to her nose. Was she checking for a snout? Blondie sighed with relief and took another bite. "These are the most hexcellent doughnuts I've ever eaten!"

Ginger smiled proudly, then looked into Camera 1. "If you want the recipe, you can crownload it on your MirrorPhone using the *Spells Kitchen* app," she said. "I'd like to thank today's special guest, Blondie Lockes."

"Scrumptious!" Blondie said, her mouth full.

Ginger waved at her virtual audience. "I hope to see you next time on *Spells Kitchen*, and remember— life is a piece of cake if you take the time to bake." Theme music rose.

"And that's a wrap," Humphrey announced. "Good show everyone." He and his crew turned off the lights, wound up the cords, then helped themselves to spelly doughnuts.

Ginger set one in a to-go box and handed it to Humphrey. "Would you give this to Hopper if you see him?"

"Sure," he said, wiping fairyberry jam from the corners of his mouth. Then Humphrey, Dexter, and the rest of the tech crew left the Cooking Class-ic Room.

Blondie sat on the edge of the counter, MirrorPad in hand. "I'll see how many live viewers you had," she said. As Blondie's fingers flew across the screen, Ginger began to clean the kitchen. She smiled as she washed the mixing bowl. Her show had been a success. No accidents, no mistakes. Everyone would want to make spelly doughnuts. A few more years at Ever After High and she'd surely be on her way to her own national show.

Blondie looked up from her MirrorPad. "Um, do you want the good news or the bad news?"

"Bad news?" Ginger froze. "What bad news?"

"Okay, I'll give you both. Good news, your doughnuts are delicious." She smiled sweetly. "Bad news... you only had five viewers."

"What?" Ginger dropped the bowl into the sink. "Five? That's gotta be a mistake." Blondie was supposed to boost ratings, but they were as low as they'd been last week.

Blondie ran her fingers over the screen, checking and rechecking. Then she looked at Ginger with a pained expression. "I'm sorry, Ginger, but as we say in the biz, your show's a flop."

Dumpty's

Doubts

A grand tree grew in the center of the Castleteria kitchen, its branches spreading across a domed ceiling, basking in sunlight. Racks of copper pans and cooking utensils hung from the walls. Pots of soup simmered on the stove, and bread turned golden brown in a large stone hearth. Cooking for the students and staff at Ever After High wasn't an easy feat, because there were so many palates to please. For example, fairies were known to have finicky appetites and preferred delicate, crustless sandwiches. Those from Wonderland insisted on hot tea with every meal. The vegetarians wanted organic salad bar options, while the Track and Shield team liked chowing down on heaping plates of barbecued ribs with smashed pumpkin.

Ginger usually loved the Farmer McGregor vegetable soup, but today she couldn't eat a bite. Her stomach felt as if it had tied itself into a pretzel knot. "I can't believe no one watched my show," she said, wiping soup steam off her glasses. She was sitting at a lunch table with Blondie. "How is that possible? Are you sure you didn't make a mistake?"

Blondie winced, looking totally insulted. "If there's one thing I know, besides getting the latest scoop, it's how to read viewership numbers." She stabbed a forkful of Ever After High pasta, which was shaped like the letters *E*, *A*, and *H*. "Obviously, having me as your guest wasn't enough to get people interested in cooking. Don't beat yourself up about it. Now and then, everyone has a bad day." While chewing, she kept her eyes peeled for signs

of clandestine activity. Her MirrorPad waited by her elbow, ready to capture anything that seemed covert.

"You've *never* had a bad day," Ginger said. "Your MirrorCast is always a success."

Blondie rested her elbows on the table and pointed her fork at Ginger. "Okay, I'll let you in on a little secret, just so you'll feel better." She leaned closer. "My numbers are down ten percent. And do you know why?" With a flick of her wrist, she pointed her fork in the opposite direction, where a group of girls sat glued to their mirror screens. Ginger slid her glasses up her nose, then craned her neck to get a peek. The girls were watching *Daring's Day*. The star of the MirrorCast was sitting at a table, eating his lunch. And even though, in real time, he was sitting in that very same Castleteria, the girls chose to watch him on their MirrorPads instead.

"He's so cute when he's eating," one of the girls said.

"Cute." Blondie rolled her eyes. Then she threw her arms in the air. "How are we supposed to compete with that?" An *E* and an *H* flew off her fork.

Ginger had no idea how to compete with cute. "Why is watching Daring eat an apple more exciting than learning how to make spelly doughnuts?" she grumbled.

Blondie stabbed another forkful of pasta. "I'll tell you why. Because Daring comes from one of the most prestigious families in fairytale history. Everyone wants to know how the other half lives." She glanced across the room.

Daring sat with a group of Royals, which included Hopper, who had apparently recovered from his morning stomachache. Many of the Royals wore crowns—the symbol of their elite status. Blondie liked to call herself a Royal, but many questioned this. There was no solid proof that her mother, Goldilocks, was a princess. But Blondie insisted. Ginger didn't judge her for trying to fit in.

Blondie retied her hair ribbon, which had begun

to droop. "I work hard every day to make my show happen, but Daring doesn't do anything. The camera simply follows him around. It's so unfair."

"Totally unfair," Ginger agreed. But she was only half talking about Daring. She couldn't help but notice that Hopper kept glancing down the Royals' table—at Briar.

"Have you ever thought of doing something else, besides baking?" Blondie asked.

"Huh?" That question cut right to Ginger's heart. "Something else? No way. My show is important to me."

"Why?" Blondie asked.

Ginger paused. She wasn't sure what to say.

"Well, I'll tell you why my show is important to me." Blondie squared her shoulders and looked right into Ginger's eyes. "I want to be a journalist. It's my calling. When I've finished my storybook destiny, I want to travel all over the kingdoms and cover the biggest news stories. When people think of news, I want them to think of me." She smiled. "I want to be the best and hardest-working journalist ever after." Then she poked Ginger in the arm. "So? Tell me the truth. Why is your show important to you?"

Ginger looked around, then spoke quietly. "Is this off the record?"

"Of course," Blondie said, putting a hand over her MirrorPad. "Off the record."

"Well, I want to be the best and hardest-working chef ever after. And when people think of delicious treats, I want them to think of me. But that won't happen if they're worried I might use an evil recipe and poison them. The show can help prove that there's another side to me other than my Candy Witch destiny."

"Then you'll have to figure out how to get more viewers," Blondie said. "And I'll help. We should stick together." Blondie looked over at the Daring fan club and scowled. "How can they *still* be watching him eat?"

Ginger stirred her soup. It was nice of Blondie to offer to help with *Spells Kitchen*. It seemed that their

MirrorCast shows had given the girls a common bond.

Blondie's blue eyes suddenly widened and she bolted to her feet. "Does it look like Apple's sharing a secret? Oooh, I'd better get over there." She grabbed her MirrorPad and dashed away.

As Ginger watched Blondie do her thing, she felt a pang of jealousy. Blondie was a natural. And though Ginger was confident in her cooking skills, she didn't have the slightest idea how to entice people to watch her show. She was hopeful that Blondie would have some good suggestions.

Humphrey walked up, carrying a lunch tray. "Hi," he said. "Can we talk?"

"Sure," Ginger replied.

Humphrey settled onto the bench across from her. After taking a long swig of fizzy water, he frowned at Ginger. "Look, I don't mean to be rude, but I heard you only got five viewers today. That's terrible."

"Yeah, I know."

The girls watching their mirror screens began to

giggle. "Oh look, Daring's squirting ketchup on his fairy fries. Isn't he adorable?"

Humphrey took another drink. "It doesn't seem fair that Daring's show is more popular than yours. But some people get all the breaks. Uh, not that I want a *break*. Get it?" He laughed so hard at his own joke that he snorted fizzy water out his nose, drenching the front of his shirt.

Ginger handed him a napkin. As Humphrey wiped his suspenders, he sighed. "I'm such a klutz. You know, sometimes I wish I could be Daring, just for one day. If I'd been Daring at the kissing booth, we'd have a dozen jars filled to the brim with cash. Who wouldn't want to be Daring?"

Ginger couldn't argue with his fantasy. Daring did have it all. Good looks, fame, fortune, destiny. He had no idea what it was like to be related to a person who frightened children. He didn't have to work for respect or popularity. He didn't have to worry about viewership. A cloud of self-pity settled over Ginger. Daring didn't have to convince people that he wasn't going to poison them! She began to stir her soup so quickly it splashed over the sides of her bowl. "Sorry," she said as she dabbed a drop off Humphrey's sleeve.

"No problem." Humphrey picked a long Hagatha hair out of his sandwich. "Anyway, Ginger, I'm afraid I have some bad news."

"More bad news?" She pushed her bowl away. "What is it?"

"Well, the Tech Club is a volunteer organization, and its members have busy schedules. Look at me, for example. I've got a full load of classes, plus hextra activities like Mathletics and Chess Club. I need to take my chicken for a walk twice a day. Not to mention the time I spend composing my rap music at Dump-T Studios." He teetered on his bench, and Ginger thought he might fall over, but he regained his balance. "The point is, Tech Club has a whole list of students waiting for help with their Mirror-Casts. If you're only getting five viewers, then we need to give our time to someone else."

Ginger couldn't believe what she was hearing. "You're quitting? But I can't do my show without the Tech Club. It's a team effort."

"*Quitting*'s not exactly the right word." Humphrey scratched his roundish head. "We just need to be fair. It doesn't make much sense for us to work on a show that no one's watching."

Blondie appeared right next to the table. Had she suddenly sprouted fairy wings and flown across the room? "I smell a scoop," she said, holding out her MirrorPad. The recording light glowed red. "What's going on?"

Humphrey smiled into the camera. "The Tech Club is going to drop Ginger's show so we can help with another show."

"Wait!" Ginger shoved her hand in front of the camera. "Don't drop me, Humphrey. Not yet. Give me another chance."

At that moment, Briar Beauty rose from the Royals' table and headed toward the exit, which took her directly past Hopper. He dropped his burger and

looked right at her. *Uh-oh*, Ginger thought. *What corny pickup line would he use today?*

"Hey, Briar," he called after clearing his throat. "If I could rearrange the alphabet, I'd put *u* and *i* closer together."

Briar stopped walking. "Hate to break it to you, Hopper, but I've heard that one before." She yawned.

"Yeah, well, my doctor says I need more vitamin B." He wagged his eyebrows.

"Ha, ha. Very funny." Briar slid her crownglasses up her forehead and looked directly at him. That momentary glance worked like a magic spell. The blush that spread across Hopper's face was as red as Red Riding Hood's cape.

Poof!

Hopper the frog fell onto the Royals' table, landing right on Daring's plate. Up to his green ankles in ketchup, he watched as Briar walked away. "Oh how my heart beats like a caged beast," he said in his mellifluous frog voice. "If only I could summon the courage to ask her on a date. But, alas, one glance from her and I am transformed." He climbed over the fairy fries, then hopped off the table and out the Castleteria door.

"Tragic," Blondie said.

The tragedy, Ginger believed, was that Hopper never used the pickup lines on her. If only he'd stop focusing on Briar and notice the pink-haired girl sitting right across the room.

"Too bad he can't talk to Briar without becoming a frog," Humphrey said with a shrug. "If Hopper were Daring for a day, he'd get the girl. No problem." A loud slurping sound filled the air as he drank more fizzy water.

Ginger reached across the table and grabbed Humphrey's arm. There was a much more important issue to deal with than Hopper's crush on Briar. "Please, Humphrey, don't quit. Give me one more chance. I can turn things around. If I get more viewers, will the Tech Club stay?"

Humphrey swallowed. Then he shrugged. "Yeah, okay. One more chance."

Science and Sorcery

ight after lunch, Ginger headed off to Science and Sorcery class. Because Ginger was the daughter of a witch, she was automatically registered for most of the "evil" classes, such as General Villainy and Home Evilnomics. But even though sorcery was often a villainous activity, all Ever After High students were required to take it.

The classroom looked like a mad scientist's laboratory, with rainbow liquids percolating in glass vials and steam rising from floor vents. There were cauldrons for brewing potions, PH strips for testing weather, and microscopes for studying microscopic dust bunnies. Ginger felt comfortable with most of the equipment, especially since the double boilers and thermometers were the same kind she used for melting chocolate. Because it involved the study of recipes, Science and Sorcery was one of her favorite classes. Unfortunately, the teacher, Professor Rumpelstiltskin, was one of her least favorite.

A nasty-tempered, gnomish man, Rumpelstiltskin spent as little time as possible instructing his students and as much time as possible punishing them. His favorite form of punishment was the pop quiz, which most often had nothing to do with science or sorcery. One day he gave a pop quiz on darning socks. Turned out he had a big hole in his own sock and wanted to find out which of his students could fix it. No one would have volunteered, on account of the professor's feet being rather hairy and unpleasant-smelling.

Rumpelstiltskin also gave hextra credit assignments

at random. If students chose not to do the assignments, however, he'd force them to climb the ladder to the classroom's attic and weave straw into gold with his magical spinning wheel. Ever After High's school board had banned Rumpelstiltskin from doing any spinning himself because of a criminal past in which he'd tried to force people to spin gold or give up their firstborn. So, by forcing his students to do the work for him, he was not *technically* defying the school board.

No one liked him. He was cranky and rude and hollered all the time. But the school administration put up with him because he possessed a vast amount of knowledge regarding science and sorcery.

Ginger sat on her assigned stool, facing the front of the classroom. The rest of the students took their places and the room fell silent. When the class bell rang, Professor Rumpelstiltskin climbed on top of his podium. Because he was only three feet tall, he got a better view from up there. He pushed his large hat from his eyes and glared at his students. His gaze settled on a girl in the back of the room. "Ms. Vood, come here!" he bellowed. There seemed to be no other setting on his vocal dial. *What does he do in a library?* Ginger wondered.

Cedar Wood walked to the front of the room and stood before the podium.

"That is gold?" he demanded, pointing to a bracelet that encircled her wrist.

Everyone knew that you should never wear gold to Rumpelstiltskin's class. And if you accidentally wore some, you should lie about it. But Cedar was incapable of lying. "Yes," she said.

"Pop quiz!" he announced with a stomp of his foot. "If you answer correctly, you get hextra credit. If you answer incorrectly, you give me gold!" This was entirely unfair, but that was how it worked in Rumpelstiltskin's class. No one ever answered the pop quizzes correctly. He pushed his sagging hat up his forehead. "Vhat is my middle name?"

"I don't know," Cedar said.

"You have three guesses!"

Though everyone liked Cedar, no one helped, because helping would result in some sort of punishment. She shrugged. "Is it Ralph? Is it Gus? Maybe Bob?"

"No, no, no!" He stomped three times. The podium wobbled. Cedar removed the bracelet and placed it in his outstretched hand. Then with a sigh, she went back to her stool.

"I forgot I was wearing it," she muttered as she passed Ginger.

Rumpelstiltskin tucked the treasure into his pocket and chuckled happily. Then he stomped again. "Open recipe book!"

Ginger eagerly turned the pages of her hextbook. She was the best in Science and Sorcery class because it often required the same skills used in cooking—measuring and mixing ingredients. But unlike Ginger's cooking, which often included improvisation and experimentation, a sorcerer's recipe was set in stone. Precision was key. When an antiheadache potion called for an ounce of stinkweed, a few leaves more could induce head swelling, and a few leaves less could induce head shrinkage. It was serious work.

"I hate lab work," the girl sitting next to Ginger whispered. Her name was Faybelle Thorn, daughter of the Dark Fairy who'd cursed Sleeping Beauty. She looked quite the opposite of Ginger. While Ginger was decorated with swirls, gumdrops, and sprinkles, Faybelle wore a dark glitter-printed tunic dress with sleeves that were covered in thorns and webbed lace. The two girls were definitely not friends, even though their families had a long tradition of mutual respect and admiration. Faybelle took her villainous bloodline very seriously. She looked down her nose at those who rebelled against their villainous destinies, including Ginger. But Faybelle had made a point of grabbing the stool next to Ginger's on the first day of class and, thus, they'd become lab partners. Ever since, she'd lazily relied on Ginger to do all the work.

Rumpelstiltskin waved his book in the air. "Today ve make boot-cleaning potion."

Hearing that the potion wasn't evil, Ginger sighed with relief. But Faybelle groaned. "Boot cleaning? Are you serious? Why?"

"Because I have dirty boots, that's vhy!"

During the remaining class time, beakers were broken, eyebrows were singed, and one student created so much foam it covered the floor. Ginger knew that mistakes were necessary when learning to cook, whether making a boot-cleaning potion or a birthday cake. She'd ruined at least a dozen batches of pixie pies before mastering the recipe. But sometimes, in the kitchen, a cooking mistake could lead in a new, exciting direction, like the time she whipped too much air into her soufflé and invented a floating cake. "What's taking you so long?" Faybelle complained as she peered over Ginger's shoulder.

"If you helped, it might go faster," Ginger said. Then she measured a single perfect drop of phoenix feather oil.

"Help?" Faybelle unfurled her wings and hovered

a foot off the floor. "Why should I help? You're the daughter of the Candy Witch. You're supposed to be an expert on following recipes." Faybelle smiled wickedly. "How about we turn it into a boot-*eating* potion and teach Rumpelstiltskin a lesson?"

"No way," Ginger said.

Faybelle made a *humph* sound. "You should start taking your legacy seriously. I heard you only got five viewers today. Poor little Ginger. Clearly, no one wants to watch you bake goodies. You should cook up a wicked goodie and feed it to someone. Now *that* would be a show worth watching."

Ginger set the beaker over a wisp of dragon flame. "I'm not interested in poisoning anyone. How many times do I have to tell you that?"

"I'm just trying to be helpful." Faybelle rose higher, then sat on the counter. She crossed her legs and started hexting on her MirrorPhone. "We daughters of the world's greatest villains should stick together."

"By sticking together, you mean I should do all the work, but you should get the credit?"

"Hexactly."

At the end of class, all the other boot-cleaning potions had proved to be failures. The potion from Apple and Cedar made Rumpelstiltskin's boots sing a happy song. "Fail!" The potion from Humphrey and Dexter made his boots ignite. "Fail!" But when Ginger placed a single droplet of her potion on each of Rumpelstiltskin's boots, the crusty leather immediately sparkled and gleamed. Ginger and Faybelle received the highest marks of the day.

The dismissal bell rang. "Another perfect grade," Faybelle said with a smirk. "I'm wickedly amazing." Then she flew out of the classroom, leaving a small cloud of fairy dust in her wake.

"You're welcome," Ginger called. She was tired of Faybelle taking advantage of her. And she was equally tired of Faybelle lecturing her about her evil destiny. Usually Ginger would try to ignore all the nasty comments that came out of the cheerhexing fairy's mouth. But one thing she'd said had actually made sense.

You should cook up a wicked goodie and feed it to someone. Now that would be a show worth watching.

Could she do such a thing? Could she stoop so low just to save *Spells Kitchen*?

Ginger waited for the classroom to clear. Then she took a deep breath. "Professor Rumpelstiltskin, may I ask you a question?"

The Desperate Deal

*N*o questions!" Rumpelstiltskin climbed off the podium and scuttled toward his desk. "Class over. You go avay!"

Even though the professor's constant bellowing made her nervous, Ginger didn't go away. She took another deep breath. "I have a MirrorCast show called *Spells Kitchen*. Have you seen it?" She hoped he would tell her that it was an amazing show and that he never missed an episode.

"No!" He climbed onto his chair and, after settling on top of a large cushion, opened a greasy paper lunch bag and began eating a cold roasted potato. Bits of burnt potato skin got stuck in his beard. She wanted to tell him that the tuber would be much tastier dipped in melted garlic butter or basted with a light elfish gravy.

"*Spells Kitchen* is my cooking show." She shuffled nervously in place. He kept eating. "Cooking is my passion, especially baking. I'm really good at it."

He narrowed his eyes at her. "Like your mother."

She shook her head. "Oh, no, not like my mother. Nothing like my mother."

"Too bad." He picked a bit of skin from his yellowed teeth. "In my day, your mother vas best cook." Was that a dreamy look filling his eyes? Were his chapped lips actually stretching into a smile? "Ve vent on date. She fed me poisoned cabbage soup and my beard exploded. It vas best date ever!"

Ew. Ginger cringed. Her horrid professor had dated

her mother? "Oh. That's nice." She shuddered. "Uh, professor, I wanted to ask you something."

"You bother me! Go avay!" He reached into the lunch bag and pulled out a lumpy green cookie. Was it covered in mold?

The last thing Ginger wanted to do was to hang out with the school's grumpiest teacher and watch him stuff his face. He hadn't used any herbs on his potato, and he hadn't bothered to frost his cookie. She could barely stand it. But she needed his help. She took a long breath. "Professor, I hate to admit this, but my MirrorCast show is an epic failure. No one is watching."

"Don't care!" Cookie bits spewed from his mouth.

"I need to cook something hexciting so people will watch." She lowered her voice. "I need a recipe that will make my next cake the most amazing cake ever eaten at Ever After High."

Rumpelstiltskin narrowed his eyes. "You need my help?"

"Yes," she said, knowing full well that it would come with a big price.

"Zen ve make deal. I give you recipe for most amazing cake ever, and you give me firstborn child!"

"What?" She cringed. "No way."

"Zen you give me all your gold!"

"I don't have any gold."

He groaned. "*Da*, okay. Let me think." He ate the rest of the cookie, then stuck a finger in the air. "I know vhat to do. I give you recipe for most amazing cake ever, and you give me...date vith your mother!"

"What?" In a million years, Ginger would have never expected such a request. She folded her arms and thought about it. Rumpelstiltskin was a vile creature, smelly and cranky, and the greediest person she'd ever met. How could she ask her mother to go on a date with him? Then again, her mother wasn't exactly popular. Men weren't lining up to take her out.

"Tell me about the recipe."

"Date first! Zen recipe."

"But how can I decide if I want the recipe or not unless I see it?"

While considering her request, Rumpelstiltskin scratched his beard. A beetle crawled out of the matted hair and scurried under his hat. "*Da*, okay. Recipe first!" He slid off the chair and waddled across the classroom to a bookshelf. After climbing a ladder, he grabbed a small roll of parchment from the top shelf. A dust cloud arose. Then he climbed back down and stood at her feet, the scroll held tightly in his hand. "This is advanced recipe! For vish cake!"

"Vish cake? What's that?"

"It make vish come true."

"Oh, *wish* cake." That sounded very interesting. She reached for the parchment, but he whipped it behind his back.

"You vant?" His hat flopped to one side.

Ginger's imagination soared. A cake that makes wishes come true would be the most amazing thing she could ever bake on her show. Students would definitely watch that episode. And the best thing was, a wish cake wasn't wicked or poisonous! "Yes, I vant. I mean, yes, I want." She held out her hand and bounced on her toes.

"Date vid Candy Vitch?" he asked, rolling the parchment between his greasy fingers.

"Professor Rumpelstiltskin?" a little voice interrupted. A small boy stuck his head out of a hole in the ceiling. Bits of straw floated down. "Can I please stop spinning straw into gold? My fingers are starting to blister."

"You spin one hour more!" Rumpelstiltskin ordered. The boy groaned, then disappeared. Ginger frowned. He was certainly the meanest teacher ever after! Maybe a date with her mother would serve him right. The Candy Witch could poison him and make all his hair fall out, or make him shrink even more so that he was the size of a rat.

"Yes," she said, her gaze fixed on the prize. "I'll get you a date with the Candy Witch." Ginger had no idea how she'd persuade her mother to accept a date with the school's worst teacher, but she'd have to make it work. Because as everyone knew, double-crossing Rumpelstiltskin was a very bad idea.

"You do not share dis recipe vith anyone. Only you make vish cake. No one else!" He handed her the scroll.

"Got it," she said. "Thanks." Then she hurried from the classroom, her heart soaring with hope.

Hocus

Pocus

When classes had finished for the day, Ginger walked to the Village of Book End, a short distance from campus. It was a lovely village, filled with delightful shops, like the Glass Slipper Shoe Store and the Mad Hatter of Wonderland's Haberdashery & Tea Shoppe. If students got tired of the Castleteria food, they could visit the Three Bears Porridge Café or the Beanstalk Bakery. But Ginger wasn't looking for shoes or a muffin. She was on a mission. She bought a hocus frappé at her favorite coffeehouse, the

Hocus Latte Café. Then she sat at the corner table where she often did her thronework. As the complex scent of coffee filled her nostrils, she opened her book bag and removed Rumpelstiltskin's parchment.

The café was busy, as usual. Apple White and Ashlynn Ella sat under a sprawling tree, happily chatting. Raven Queen sat by herself, taking notes from a hextbook. A Chemythstry study group had gathered around one of the big tables. The students were practicing for an upcoming quiz. Though the noise level was fairly loud, Ginger didn't let it distract her. She had only one thing on her mind—saving *Spells Kitchen*.

She cleaned her glasses with a tissue, then, after a long, cool sip of her frappé, she unrolled the parchment. There'd been no time to read it until now. And until she read it, she wasn't going to call her mother and beg her to go on a pity date with Rumpelstiltskin. The recipe had to be good before she'd put her mother in such an unpleasant situation. Fairy, fairy good.

Here's what she discovered:

A Little Wish Cake

A thimble-sized cake infused with a wishing spell

Warning: This recipe should not be attempted by unseasoned cooks. Only those skilled in the art of baking should venture forth.

The following rules apply to the wish cake:

*Each chef is allowed to create one wish cake during his/her lifetime. Any attempts to bake additional wish cakes will result in inedible lumps and burnt fingers.

*The wish cake cannot be eaten by its creator. If the chef eats the cake and attempts to make a wish, the spell will evaporate.

Ginger realized that she hadn't even considered using the wish on herself. That could have been fun. She could have wished that *Spells Kitchen* was the most watched show in all the kingdoms. Or she

could have wished that no one would ever again lecture her about her wicked heritage. Or worry that she might bake something evil.

She took another sip, then continued reading. The cake recipe was mostly ordinary, calling for flour, sugar, butter, eggs, and some baking powder. The wishing potion was the difficult aspect, requiring skill and patience. It contained ingredients she'd seen in her mother's pantry many times, like pumpkin seed oil, syrup of serpent, and ground unicorn horn. The trick was to distill the potion down to a single drop. Nothing more, nothing less. *I can do that*, Ginger thought. However, the final instructions were a bit confusing.

Wish Rules:

* To activate the wish spell, the entire cake must be eaten, then the wish must be spoken aloud.

* The wish cannot be big, such as conquering a kingdom or world domination.

* *It cannot involve other people, such as a revenge plot.*

* *It cannot involve illegal activity, such as cheating on a test or stealing treasure.*

* *The wish must be little.*

A *little* wish? That didn't sound very dramatic. Ginger slumped in her chair. How was she supposed to draw viewers to her show if her guest wished for a new pair of shoes or a different eye color? And did she really want to ask her mom to do a huge favor for something that yielded only a *little* wish?

"Hello, fellow fairytales," a familiar voice chirped. Everyone in the Hocus Latte Café turned to look at the large mirror mounted on the central tree. Blondie's perky face and cascading curls filled the screen. "Be sure to watch tonight's episode of *Just Right* to find out if the following fables are true or false. Is Apple White planning a surprise party for a certain charming prince?" From across the café, at

her table, Apple giggled. "Is Raven Queen thinking about trading her dragon for a kitten?"

Raven looked up from her hextbook. "That is totally false," she said with a scowl.

Blondie continued. "And is Ginger Breadhouse about to say 'The End' to *Spells Kitchen*? Be sure to watch tonight's episode for the answers to these latest scoops. Remember, if it's not too hot or too cold, it's just right!"

The screen went dark and the students returned to their conversations. Ginger heard a few of them say, "What's *Spells Kitchen*?"

Unbelievable. If her show disappeared, no one would even notice!

"Sorry about your show," a voice said. Melody Piper took the seat opposite Ginger's.

"There's no need to be sorry," Ginger told her. "It's not over yet."

"That's the attitude. Hey, whatcha reading?" Melody slid her headphones away from her ears. "It looks old."

"It's a recipe," Ginger said. She turned the parchment facedown.

"I could have guessed that." Melody stirred whipped cream into her caramel frappé. "Why are you hiding it? I'm not Blondie. I'm not going to tell everyone."

It was true that Melody was way better at keeping secrets than Blondie. To be fair, almost *anyone* was better at keeping secrets. Ginger glanced around. Then she whispered, "It's a special recipe."

"Special?" Blondie suddenly appeared and plopped herself into the other empty chair. "What's special?"

"How do you do that?" Melody asked. "Seriously? It's like you hear people whispering and appear out of thin air. Do you have a magic eavesdropping charm or something?"

"There's no magic," Blondie said proudly. "Being a journalist is hard work. I have to constantly be on the lookout. It's exhausting." She smiled. "But in this case it was pure coincidence. I was coming over to see you guys. So? What's this special thing you're

whispering about?" She wiggled in the chair. "Come on, spill it!"

Ginger knew it was impossible to keep anything from Blondie. Besides, she needed her friend's advice. "Well, as you know, I have to get more viewers or the Tech Club will drop me. So I decided I'd better do something hexciting." She paused, then pushed her glasses up her nose. "Don't freak out, but I asked Rumpelstiltskin for a special recipe."

Blondie gasped. "You're not going to poison someone, are you?"

"Of course not. Have you flipped your crown?" Ginger sat back and tightly folded her arms. "Why do people always ask me that?"

"I'm a journalist. It's a reasonable question. You're the daughter of the Candy Witch."

"It's *not* a reasonable question." A wave of hurt washed over Ginger. She fought back tears as best as she could. All those unhappy memories from spellementary school resurfaced. "Haven't I proved that I'm *not* my mom? What do I have to do to make everyone stop stereotyping me?" She swept her pink ponytails behind her shoulders, then wagged a finger at Blondie. "How would you feel if everyone thought you were exactly like *your* mom? She broke into the bears' cottage and snooped around, uninvited." Ginger's hand fell to her lap. She stopped talking. Blondie was *exactly* like her mom. Bad example. Ginger sighed. "I'm so tired of trying to prove that I'm my own person."

"I'm royally sorry," Blondie said, her voice quiet and sincere. "I didn't mean to hurt your feelings. You *are* your own person. You're Ginger Breadhouse, pastry chef extraordinaire." She hugged Ginger. Then Melody hugged Ginger. As Ginger wiped tears from her eyes, the bad feelings drifted away. She was so lucky to have such good friends.

Blondie looked around, then rapped her fingers on the upside-down parchment. "Now, will you show me what Rumpelstiltskin gave you?"

"Yeah, show us," Melody said. The girls leaned on the table, their eyes wide with wonder.

"Okay." Ginger looked around cautiously to make sure no one else was eavesdropping. "You know how people blow out candles on their birthday cakes and make a wish?" The girls nodded. "Well, I have a recipe for a little wish cake. You eat the cake, make a wish, and it actually comes true."

"Oh. My. Wand!" Blondie said. "Seriously?"

"If I bake the wish cake on my show and feed it to a special guest, do you think I'd get more viewers?"

"I want to do it," Melody said, scrambling out of her chair. "Can I do it? Please? Make me your special guest. I already know my wish. I want to own a nightclub and be the DJ and play all my favorite music and—"

"Wait a spell, I want to do it," Blondie interrupted. "Make me your special guest. I want my own nationally syndicated talk show."

Melody narrowed her eyes. "I'm her roommate. She should choose me."

Blondie got to her feet and squared her shoulders. "I'm her friend. The choice is obvious."

Ginger wasn't surprised that they looked ready to wrestle each other. Who wouldn't jump at the chance to make her dreams come true? "I hate to break it to you, but you can't wish for fame. Or fortune. You can't wish for anything big. It has to be a *little* wish."

"A *little* wish?" they said at the same time.

"The wish spell only grants a little wish." Ginger shrugged. "I guess it's to protect people, you know, so you can't affect other people's lives in a bad way. Maybe you could wish for a new MirrorPad or some new music."

"Who wants to waste a magical wish on that kind of stuff?" Melody asked. She sighed with disappointment, then sank back into her chair.

"I don't think a *little* wish is going to save your show," Blondie said matter-of-factly. She arranged her golden curls, then sat down. "Unless you get the Evil Queen herself to be your guest, or someone equally controversial."

Kissing sounds rose above the coffeehouse chatter.

Ginger glanced across the café. Hopper had just walked in, dressed in his usual shorts and embroidered jacket. Two guys from the Track and Shield team were teasing him by blowing kisses his way. "Yeah, yeah, very funny," Hopper said with a wave. "The kissing booth was a dumb idea. I get it. Let's turn the page already!" He stepped up to the counter. "Hey, good-looking," he said to the barista. "How about one latte for me, and another latte for you, and then we can latte our way outta here." He leaned real close to her and winked.

"Uh, no thanks," the girl said.

Ginger cringed. As usual, Hopper was using a stupid pickup line. And, *as usual*, he hadn't even noticed that she was sitting just a few feet away.

"If you change your mind, just give me a ring," he told the barista. "My number is 1-800-You-Don't-Know-What-You're-Missing."

Ginger rolled her eyes. That hadn't even made sense. Poor Hopper. Why did he try so hard with all the other girls on the planet when the perfect girl was sitting right there? He didn't need to pretend to be cool around Ginger. If only he'd notice her and give her a chance. Then she realized something— she'd missed her opportunity to get his attention at the kissing booth, but she wasn't going to miss this new opportunity. As Hopper grabbed his latte and left the Hocus Latte Café, Ginger turned to Blondie and Melody. "What if I made Hopper my guest and let him eat the wish cake?"

"Instead of us?" Melody frowned. "But who wants to watch Hopper?"

"I'd watch him," Ginger said defensively.

Melody laughed. "Well, of course *you'd* watch him. You've got a mad crush on him."

Had it been that obvious? Ginger thought she'd hidden her feelings.

"I think Hopper's a bad choice for a guest," Blondie said. "The boys like him well enough, but he's not popular with the girls."

"That's only because he doesn't know how to talk to girls," Ginger explained.

"He's the absolute worst at talking to girls." Blondie frowned. "I can't believe I'm going to say this, but if you want to have a boy as a guest, you should ask the most popular boy. Everyone would watch your MirrorCast if Daring Charming made an appearance."

"Daring doesn't need a wish cake. He already has everything he wants. Besides, I don't want Daring to be my guest. I want Hopper." She grabbed her cauldron purse.

"I think you're making a huge mistake," Blondie called as Ginger hurried away.

Frog Talk

Ginger was amazed at how nervous she felt as she charged out of the Hocus Latte Café, the wish cake recipe tucked into her book bag. She'd talked to Hopper a few times before, but never about anything as important as being a guest star, or saving a MirrorCast show. A sinking feeling filled her stomach, reminding her of a deflating soufflé. Why was she so jittery?

Because you like him, she told herself.

Why did it have to be this way? Why did having

a crush make her feel as if her legs were made of pudding? Beads of sweat arose on her forehead. *Yeesh.* Having a secret crush was like having the flu!

Her ponytails bounced as she hurried over the cobblestones, past the Beanstalk Bakery and the Gingerbread Boutique. Hopper was a few minutes ahead of her. If she ran, she could catch up before he reached campus. Then she stopped in her tracks. Up ahead, Hopper stood in the middle of the lane, watching as Briar Beauty walked right toward him. Briar was busy hexting on her MirrorPhone, so she hadn't noticed that he was in her path. His whole body stiffened.

"Uh, hey, Briar." His voice cracked. He rubbed the back of his neck. Was he sweating, too? Was his stomach tight? Why couldn't he feel that way about Ginger instead of Briar? Then, at least, they'd both be miserable at the same time.

But it made sense that he was drawn to Briar. They were both Royals, after all. Her fairytale story was to fall asleep and be saved by a prince. His was to turn into a frog and be saved by a princess. Ginger had no prince in her story. And she certainly wasn't a princess.

Sometimes, life was so unfair!

She darted behind a carriage hitching post and watched as the awkward encounter proceeded. Trying to look relaxed, Hopper leaned against a tree, but he misjudged the angle and his shoulder slipped. Trying to recover from the stumble, he changed position and leaned with the other shoulder. Then he opened his mouth. *Uh-oh*, Ginger thought. *Here it comes.*

"I'm not a photographer, Briar, but I can sure picture us together."

Briar glanced up from her phone, but only for a second. "Oh, hey, Hopper." Then she went right back to hexting. Without a doubt, she had as little interest in Hopper as Hopper seemed to have in Ginger.

But Briar's glance was all it took to make Hopper blush.

Poof!

Hopper the frog fell onto the cobblestones. "Bye," Briar said. Then she carefully stepped over him and continued into town.

Maybe this was a good turn of events. It would be easier to talk to Hopper the frog. At least he could put words together and form a sentence that wasn't a pickup line.

As soon as Briar was out of view, Ginger marched up the lane, then stood over the royal frog. He sat on a stone, his miniature crown perched on his green head. His latte cup had landed next to him. It was more than twice his size. "Hopper?"

He glanced upward. "Indeed, fair damsel, it is I." He rose onto his back legs and bowed. "Prince Hopper Croakington the Second at your service." For such a small creature, his voice boomed, as if he were performing on a Shakespearean stage. It was amazing how much dignity he mustered when in amphibian form.

Ginger's heartbeat returned to normal. She didn't feel nervous, because her crush was on Hopper the boy, not on Hopper the frog. It was as if she were talking to an entirely different being. They shared the same brain, maybe, but the boy and the frog were total opposites.

"Hopper, I need to ask you something." It felt weird towering over him. If she suddenly tripped, he'd get squished! "Uh, can I pick you up?"

"The honor would be entirely mine."

She knelt and offered her hand. As he stepped onto her palm, she shivered. Those little webbed feet were cold. Once he'd settled, she stood and held him in front of her face. As she looked into his bulbous eyes, she felt a pang of guilt. How many times had she found frog eyeballs floating in her mother's cauldron? If he ever transformed in front of the Candy Witch, he'd be toast. Scratch that. He'd be frog leg soup!

"I wanted to ask you if you'd be on my MirrorCast show," she said, trying to erase from her mind the horrid image of Hopper stew.

"Your show?" He blinked. "Ah, yes, you are

referring to your delightful yet unappreciated entertainment venture. I am flattered by the invitation, and I assure you that though my stature be diminutive and amphibious, I am capable of wooing an audience. However, have you considered the possible consequences?"

"What do you mean?" she asked.

"It is my unfortunate curse to turn back into human form without notice. While I would make an excellent guest, due to my extensive vocabulary and rapier wit, in boy form I am an embarrassing lunk, incapable of holding a decent conversation with the opposite gender."

True, but you sure are a lot cuter as a boy, Ginger thought.

"It doesn't really matter to me whether you're Hopper the boy or Hopper the frog," she said. "I'm going to bake something special. I just need you to be there."

He tensed. Then his round eyes narrowed to slits. "Forgive me for asking . . . but you wouldn't, perchance, be baking something *poisonous*? Or *frog du jour*?"

Ginger groaned. Even frogs suspected her. "No, of course not. I want you to be my *guest*, not my main dish! I'm going to bake a wish cake. If you eat it, you can make a wish and it will actually come true."

"Hark, did I hear correctly?" A huge grin spread from earhole to earhole. "A wish?" Ginger nodded. He stood on his hind legs and raised his little arms to the sky. "Shall I wish for a trip to the moon, or a handful of starlight to keep in my pocket? Shall I rule a lily pad kingdom or command the insects to serve at my beck and call?"

Wow, he had some grand dreams.

"Sorry, but the wish can't be that big. It has to be something smaller." Her hand suddenly felt heavy, as if she were carrying a brick.

Poof!

The frog disappeared and Hopper was standing next to her, his right foot on top of hers. "Oops. Sorry about that," he said, stepping away. His voice was back to its normal range. As he reached down to grab his latte, she quickly wiped some slime off her hand. "So, uh, about that wish. What do you mean it has to be *smaller*?"

"Well, I know you're new to Tech Club and you haven't been on the *Spells Kitchen* set yet, since you had that stomachache earlier, but the truth is..." She paused. "I only got five viewers today."

"Yikes," he said. "That's brutal."

"Yep, brutal." She couldn't have chosen a more fitting word. "Anyway, I'm trying to get students to watch *Spells Kitchen*. I thought I could make you my special guest and have you eat the wish cake."

"Yeah, about that..." He rubbed the back of his neck again. "I don't really want to command an insect army, or put starlight in my pocket. I say weird things when I'm a frog."

You say weird things when you're a person, too. "Well then, what would you wish for?" she asked. *Don't say Briar. Please don't say Briar.*

He glanced around. They were alone on the path.

Then he looked right into Ginger's eyes. She almost melted. "I get nervous around girls. I always have. It's tough, you know, because I'm roommates with Daring, and all he has to do is open our door and girls come running. He has no trouble talking to them. But I can barely say hello."

She smiled encouragingly. "You're talking to me right now, and you don't seem nervous."

"I know. For some reason, you don't make me feel nervous. It's like I don't need to prove anything to you."

"What do you have to prove?"

"That I'm as good as the other princes. I mean, I know I'm handsome and smart and athletic, but what does any of that matter if I'm always turning into a frog? Girls aren't crazy about frogs, believe me. Why couldn't I turn into a dragon, or a racehorse, or something that's not slimy? When girls look at me, all they see is frog boy."

"Maybe some girls," Ginger said. "But not all." *That's not what I see.*

"Well, Briar does. And as long as I turn into a frog every time I try to talk to her, I don't stand a chance at getting a date with her."

Yep, he definitely had Briar on the brain.

For a moment, Ginger was tempted to choose a different special guest for her show. Because the last thing she wanted was to act as a matchmaker for Hopper and Briar! But he suddenly looked so sad, as if the rejection he'd felt over the years was hitting him all at once—like a big, fat punch to the gut. Ginger knew exactly how he felt. There'd been many times when she'd watched kids walk past her front window on their way to school. She'd wave through the glass, but they'd point at the house, squeal, and run away.

What Ginger was beginning to understand was that rejection was one of life's ingredients. It wasn't a necessity, like eggs are for a fluffy thronecake, or lard is for a perfectly flaky crust, but it had the power to build character or to knock it down. Though Ginger had claimed her own identity in as loud a way as she possibly could, she still struggled with people who judged her based on her family's history. Likewise, while Hopper acted the part of a confident prince, he still felt judged by girls who saw him only as a frog boy.

Ginger wouldn't choose another guest. Because someone had once told Ginger that if you truly care about someone, you want that someone to be happy.

"Why don't you come on my show? You could wish to talk to girls without turning into a frog," she said. That sounded like a smallish wish. "I bet that would work."

"That would be great!" His eyes lit up, and he beamed such a bright smile it could have competed with Daring's. "If I could talk to girls, then that would mean I could talk to Briar! I'd have a chance with her!"

And there it was. He didn't care about talking to *girls*. Just to one girl. Ginger sighed.

"I'll do it!" he said. Then he playfully punched her in the shoulder, the way he might punch Daring or

Sparrow. "Thanks, Ginger. You're the best!" As he sauntered off, Ginger lingered in his left-behind scent of expensive soap and coffee. She felt a bit woozy. A shoulder punch wasn't exactly a hug, but for now it would do.

Sure, Hopper was going to be on her show just to get another girl's attention, but she decided not to worry about that. It was more important for her to think about saving *Spells Kitchen*. Everyone at school knew that Hopper turned into a frog whenever he talked to Briar. Who wouldn't want to watch his wish come true? Her viewership numbers would soar!

Besides, she could try to win him over at a later date.

As she slung her cauldron purse over her shoulder, she smiled. Everything was in order—her special guest and her special recipe. What could go wrong?

Mommy

Makeover

As a little girl, Ginger often wondered what it would be like to be a member of a royal family. To be raised in a castle, with a bevy of servants, a closet full of gowns, and evenings spent at feasts and balls. She also wondered what it would be like to be born into an ordinary family, with parents who worked as carriage drivers, shopkeepers, or teachers. But most of all, what it would be like to not have people scream in terror when her mother walked into a room.

After finishing kingdergarten at home, Ginger

worked up the courage to go back to school. She knew that with her new talent as a baker, she could win friends. But it was very important that she appeared to be "normal."

"But, sweetie pie, normal is boring," her mother said. "Normal should be against the law."

"I just want to fit in," Ginger told her. "Can I have a Cinderella lunch box?"

"Why would you want such a thing? Why don't you pack your lunch in an old boot, the way all wicked witches do?"

"Because everyone at school carries a lunch box."

"If everyone jumped off a cliff, would you?" her mother asked.

"That's ridiculous," Ginger said. "Jumping off a cliff is stupid. Fitting in is important."

The next few years of school were a success for Ginger. Hiding her witchy roots was a constant struggle, but she managed. She never volunteered her mother to bring snacks, or be recess mom, or carriagepool mom. She continued to make her own nonpoisoned goodies, and they were the top sellers at the school bake sales. She didn't invite anyone to her house, for fear they'd discover the truth. Soon, she was once again included in playdates and parties.

But then came a day she'd never forget. It was almost time for her graduation from middle school. She stood in line with the other students to receive her black graduation cap and gown. "Here's your ticket," Principal John Thumb said, handing Ginger a single yellow ticket. "According to our records, you have one parent and no siblings. So give this ticket to your parent so that he or she may attend the graduation ceremony."

"Thank you," Ginger mumbled as she took the ticket.

As she walked home, she imagined the scene. The Grimmnasium would be filled to the brim with proud parents and grandparents, all applauding and cheering as students crossed the stage, accepting their diplomas. But when Ginger took her diploma, no smiling parent would be watching her. And when the ceremony was over, no one would be waiting with flowers.

Because how could she invite the Candy Witch to school? After all the years of hiding her identity, how could she let everyone know the truth?

As she walked home, rain pelted her face and soaked through her robe. She threw open the front door to her house. "How was your day?" the Candy Witch asked. She was in the kitchen, stewing the tail of a rat.

Ginger crumpled the ticket and tossed it into the trash. "Fine," she said, kicking off her galoshes.

The Candy Witch reached into the trash, picked out the ticket, and read it. "'Admit one.' Why are you throwing this away?"

Ginger's eyes filled with tears. She loved her mother, and she'd wanted to share this special day with her. But at the same time, she'd been trying to protect herself from the judgment of others. "It's so unfair!" she said. Then she ran up to her room and fell upon her bed in a heap of misery and confusion.

he next morning, the Candy Witch announced that she had an important appointment and wanted Ginger to join her. To Ginger's surprise, they ended up at a beauty parlor.

"Make me presentable," the witch told the beautician, "so that I can attend my daughter's graduation without terrifying everyone."

Ginger couldn't believe what she was hearing. "Why are you doing this?" she asked.

"Because, honey bunny, I love you. And if you care about someone, then you want that someone to be happy." She patted her daughter's head, then sat in the vinyl seat. "I must admit, I've been set in my ways. I'm proud of my witchy appearance. But, clearly, others do not appreciate it and you should not have to suffer."

"But, Mom, I don't want you to change who you are. I just want people to stop judging you." She lowered her gaze. "I mean, judging *us*."

"Well, that's not going to happen. So the only way to tackle this problem is for me to try to fit in. At least on the outside."

Ginger had wished, time and time again, to have a normal-looking parent so the kids at school wouldn't freak out. But now that it was really happening, she felt worried.

"This is gonna take all day," the beautician complained as she tried to run a brush through the Candy Witch's tangled green hair. "You got twigs in here." She shrieked as something blinked at her. "Oh my godmother, is that a toad?" The toad leaped off the witch's head. Ginger opened the front door so it could hop to freedom.

"I've never seen such a mess," the beautician commented as her comb broke in two. "Haven't you ever heard of conditioner?"

The Candy Witch narrowed her eyes. Then she pulled a piece of candy from her pocket. "Would you like a snackypoo, dearie?"

"Mother!" Ginger cried, wrenching the candy from

her mother's grip. "If you poison her, she won't be able to do her job."

The witch shrugged. "You're right. My bad."

As Ginger tossed the candy into a wastebasket, it sizzled and popped. Then she settled onto the sofa, with a stack of well-read magazines to keep her occupied.

"Your daughter's pink hair is so beautiful," the beautician said. "Where did it come from?"

"Apparently, it's a recessive gene," the Candy Witch grumbled.

The beautician worked all day, washing, clipping, plucking, shaving, coloring, and spritzing. Ginger eventually fell asleep, but she awoke to someone tapping her shoulder. "Where's my mom?" she asked, rubbing her eyes and looking around.

"I'm right here."

Ginger couldn't believe it. "Mom? Is that really you?"

A very lovely lady sat in the same chair where a witch had sat earlier. Her long hair was pink and silky, like Ginger's, and it was pulled off her face with a white ribbon. Her eyelashes were curled and her eyelids sparkled with blue shadow. The only recognizable feature was the wart, which still sat on her chin. However, its black wiry hair was missing.

"You'll have to come in for weekly maintenance," the beautician said as she took out her appointment calendar. "I'll put you down for next Tuesday. What's your name?"

Ginger cringed. *Don't say it. Don't say it.*

"My name is..." She cackled. "Why, dearie, my name is Ms. Breadhouse."

The next morning brought a brief rain shower to Ever After High, just enough to keep the grass green and the flowers supple. After the clouds drifted away, the sun went to work, gently waking the school with its warm embrace. Because it was Saturday, most students chose to sleep in. Thus, breakfast was served at a later hour. After eating hot cross buns, Ginger and Melody settled at their desks to study. Melody disappeared behind her headphones as she worked on Muse-ic Theory thronework. Ginger fed the pair of guppies that shared the fish tank with Jelly. Jelly, being a magical candy fish, didn't need to eat. Then, just as Ginger began to memorize the wish cake recipe, her MirrorPhone buzzed.

It was a hext from Professor Rumpelstiltskin.

Vhat time is date?

Weird. He even hexted with an accent.

Ginger groaned. She couldn't put this off much longer. She had to call her mother and ask her for this horrid favor. She checked to make sure Melody was distracted by music, then she carried her phone into her closet and shut the door. She wanted privacy for this particular conversation. After turning on the overhead light, she pushed aside shoes and hats and sat on the carpet. Then she dialed her mother's number. It rang five times before the familiar voice answered. "Hello, sweetie pie, so nice to hear from you." Her mother appeared on the MirrorChat screen.

"Hi, Mom." Though the makeover had happened

a while ago, Ginger still wasn't used to seeing her mom with pink hair and eyeliner. But she wasn't looking quite right. "Uh, is that a false eyelash on your cheek?"

Ms. Breadhouse flicked the lash away. "It takes so much energy to put on all that makeup every morning," she said with a sigh. "I'm having trouble keeping up with the beauty routine." Ginger noticed that green roots were showing along the part in her mother's hair and that her mom's fingernails were ragged again.

"Mom, you don't have to—"

"How's school?" Ms. Breadhouse asked. A raven cawed in the background.

"Fine." Ginger paused, then peeked out a crack in the closet door. Melody was still plugged into her music, tapping her feet to the rhythm. Ginger scooted to the back of the closet until she was hidden behind a long winter coat. "Uh, Mom, there's something I need to ask you."

"What's that, smoochy-poochy?"

"I made a deal with . . . *Rumpelstiltskin*."

Ms. Breadhouse gasped. "You didn't promise him your firstborn, did you?"

"No. But I kinda promised him a date with you."

Long, drawn-out silence hissed through the phone. Ginger cringed. Surely her mother was angry. Surely she'd refuse. But when she finally spoke, her voice was very matter-of-fact. "I don't need your help finding a date, dearie. I filled out my personal statement with a new nonwitchy dating site. Listen to this: 'Seeking a companion who enjoys old-fashioned cooking, with no unexpected allergic reactions or unusual side effects.'" She frowned. "Does that sound normal?"

"Yeah, I guess so."

"It sounds so boring to me. Everyone wants to have romantic dinners and take long walks at sunset. What about a nice hike through a swamp? Or a trip to the emergency room? Now, that's a date!"

"Mom?" The thing Ginger was about to confess felt so heavy she sank against the closet wall. "I still need you to go on a date with Rumpelstiltskin. My MirrorCast show is a failure. No one is watching."

"I'm watching. And our neighbor is watching, that old woman who lives in a shoe."

"Thanks, Mom, but my crew is going to quit if I don't do something to get more people to watch."

"What does Rumpelstiltskin have to do with this?"

"I asked him for a special recipe."

"You what? Why didn't you come to me for a special recipe? I have more special recipes than I can count."

"Yes, but I don't want to poison anyone on my show."

"I see. Sticking to the whole 'I don't want to be a wicked witch' thing." Ms. Breadhouse sighed. "I keep hoping you'll change your mind."

"Rumpelstiltskin gave me a recipe for wish cake. The special potion infuses the cake with a wishing spell. I'm sure I can get a lot of viewers with a recipe like that. But he wanted something in return." Ginger held the phone closer and lowered her voice

to a whisper. She really didn't want anyone to overhear the next sentence. "Apparently, you two *dated*?"

The Candy Witch shrugged. "Did we? That was a very long time ago. Who can remember the details?"

"He remembers. And he loves your cooking."

"Really?" She cackled with surprise. "Nobody *loves* my cooking."

"In exchange for the wish cake recipe, I promised that you'd go on another date. Could you cook him something?" Ginger stared into the phone. "Please?"

"I'm curious, Ginger pie. Who have you chosen to eat the wish cake?"

"Hopper Croakington the Second."

"A boy?" She smiled. "Do you like this boy?"

Ginger shook her head. "N-no. It's n-not like that." But even on the phone's small screen, her blush revealed the truth. "Okay, so I like him a little. He's . . . nice."

Ms. Breadhouse reached into the pantry and grabbed a picnic basket. "For my daughter, who wants to give a wish to the boy she likes, I will cook a meal

for Rumpelstiltskin—a meal he'll never forget." She cackled so loudly it echoed off the closet walls.

"Thanks, Mom." Ginger was about to hang up, but something was bothering her. "Mom?"

"Yes?"

"Do you still like your makeover? I mean, I'm at boarding school now, and everyone here already knows that I'm your daughter. So there's no reason to keep hiding your true appearance."

"But, sweetie pie, if I come to visit you at school, isn't it better if I look like this? You don't want all the children fleeing in terror, do you?"

"I guess not, but—"

"Then it's settled. Well, I'd better get to work on this gourmet picnic for Rumpy. Bye."

"Bye." The screen went black. Ginger had noted a touch of sadness in her mom's voice. She'd ask her mother about it the next time they spoke. For now, everything was falling into place. The recipe, the guest, a special lunch for Rumpelstiltskin. Ginger

felt lighter, as if all her worries had floated away. She opened the closet door.

Faybelle Thorn's wicked smile greeted her.

"Just so you know," Faybelle said, "I heard *every-thing.*"

Fairy

Blackmail

aybelle Thorn's wings beat the air, casting a breeze throughout the dorm room. She wore a midnight-blue shimmering tunic and high-top sneakers. Her cheerhexing pom-poms stuck out of her sequined book bag. She hovered a couple of feet above the carpet, a smirk spread across her face. "Of all the princes to be crushing on, why would you choose Hopper Croakington? He's so...slimy."

"He's not slimy," Ginger said. "Well, maybe a little when he's a frog, but I *don't* have a crush on him."

Faybelle's eyes were like pools of glacier water, and they stared coldly at Ginger. "I heard you admit it."

Ginger glanced across the room at Melody. Her roommate was hunched over her desk, still wearing her headphones. She apparently hadn't noticed that Faybelle had invaded their room. "You shouldn't listen to other people's conversations," Ginger told the fairy. "It's rude."

"Rude is what I do." She folded her arms. "Rude is what we're *both* supposed to do. We're the daughters of villains. Our families have been friends for generations. Why do I have to keep reminding you of that?"

Ginger groaned. She didn't want to have another discussion about how she was supposed to follow in her mother's bootsteps. She closed the closet door. "Well, I'm kinda busy," she said, hoping Faybelle would take the hint and leave. But the fairy continued to hover. She wanted something.

"It doesn't seem fair that Professor Grumpy-pants gave you a special recipe. What about the rest of us?"

"If you want a special recipe, go ask for one," Ginger said.

"I don't want *hextra* work." Faybelle rolled her eyes. Then she flew backward and settled on the edge of Ginger's bed, her wings folding behind her. "I'm way too busy with cheerhexing practice, and I need to update my evil blog and hold a meeting of the Villain Club. You should join, by the way."

"No thanks." Once upon a time, Ginger would have been thrilled to be invited to join a club—any club.

Faybelle pulled a silver comb from her pocket and ran it through her shimmery blond hair. "I'll never understand why you insist on being like those Rebels who want to change their destinies."

Ginger hadn't officially declared herself a Rebel. And even if she had, which she hadn't, it was none of Faybelle's business! She pointed toward the hallway. "I think you should go. I've got stuff to work on."

"Yeah, like that show of yours that no one

watches." Faybelle smirked. Ginger's arm fell to her side. Hearing someone else say it made it all the worse. Faybelle tucked her comb away. "I'm here to make you an offer. You know the saying—you help me and I don't make your life miserable?"

Ginger glared through her glasses. "Uh, actually, the saying is, you help me, I help you."

"Not in my book." Faybelle unfurled her wings and rose off the bed. Fairy dust drifted onto Ginger's quilt. "Here's my offer. If you let me eat the wish cake, then I won't tell everyone that you're madly crushing on Hopper."

"That's so rotten."

"Thank you."

At that moment, Apple White stepped into the room. "Hello, everyone," she said in her cheerful-as-usual voice. As she smiled, two perfect dimples appeared on her cheeks. "I just got a care package from my parents. Look!" She held up a basket filled with red apples. "The first of the season."

The flash of red must have caught Melody's

attention because she took off her headphones. "Hey, what's going on?"

"One for you," Apple said, handing a piece of fruit to Melody. Then she handed one to Faybelle and another to Ginger. "Remember, a healthy villain is a happy villain. Charm you later," she called as she hurried off to make more deliveries.

"What are *you* doing in our room?" Melody asked as she looked up at Faybelle.

"Calm down, Piper. I'm not staying long." Faybelle took a bite of the apple. Then she flew very close to Ginger. "So? Are you going to let me eat the wish cake?" Her lips glistened with apple juice.

Ginger stuck out her chin. "You're too late. I've already chosen Hopper."

Faybelle's wings began to beat furiously. She threw the apple across the room. It bounced off the wall and nearly broke a mirror. "You're going to re-gret this, Ginger Breadhouse!" Then she flew out of the room, leaving a choking cloud of fairy dust in her wake.

A Wonderful Wish Day

The next morning, Ginger woke up early, her stomach jittery. This was her last chance to prove to the Tech Club that she deserved its help. And that she could bake delicious things that could bring happiness and change people's lives.

And that she didn't want to poison anyone! That was important, too.

She chose one of her prettiest outfits—a modern chef's jacket with gumdrop buttons and waffle-cone accents. She pulled her pink hair into two ponytails and sprinkled them with glitter. Then she cleaned her pink glasses until they sparkled. Then, for the final pièce de résistance, she set a chocolate cupcake chef's hat on her head. It was an ensemble fit for a spellebrity chef.

Sunday was the perfect day to record the MirrorCast since none of the students had classes. Blondie had made sure to spread the word for her. She'd hexted the entire student body, calling the event "A Wonderful Wish Day."

The halls were buzzing. "Is it true?" Apple asked. "Are you going to help Hopper so he won't turn into a frog when he talks to Briar?"

"That's the plan," Ginger told her.

Raven stopped Ginger in the hallway. Her iridescent black dress shimmered in the chandelier light. "Just thought you should know that Faybelle's telling everyone you have a secret crush on Hopper."

"Huh?" Ginger shook her head. "Whatever do you mean? He's nice, but I don't like him *that* way."

"You don't have to prove anything to me," Raven said with a shrug. She was one of the least judgmental people Ginger had ever met, probably because Raven was usually the one being judged. "Good luck with your show."

"Thanks." There was no time to worry about Faybelle and her wicked intentions. Ginger refused to start this day off on the wrong slipper. She hurried from the dormitory, Rumpelstiltskin's parchment tucked carefully into her pocket. She'd memorized the recipe but wanted to have it, just in case nerves muddled her brain. Baking a cake on her show was one thing, but baking a cake for Hopper *and* trying to save her show at the same time was going to be a challenge. Her heart was bouncing around like a jumping bean.

Daring stood in the courtyard, his groupies and reality show camera crew surrounding him. As he smiled, the glow of his teeth set someone's paper latte cup on fire. Then he waved at Ginger. "I'll be watching your show!"

Wow, Ginger thought. Daring Charming rarely said more than two words to her. And if he was going to watch her show, that meant that all his groupies would be watching, too. "Thanks," she called back.

"Ms. Breadhouse!"

Ginger stopped in her tracks. Headmaster Grimm stood before her, his hands clasped behind his back. He was an imposing figure, tall and proud, with thick gray hair and an authoritative voice. "I understand that you intend to bake a cake that contains a magical potion during your MirrorCast show this morning."

"That's right," she said with a gulp. The headmaster always made Ginger feel a bit nervous. He had very strong opinions about what students should and should not do. He believed in tradition and following one's predetermined story. Thus, he did not approve of the Rebels, or of anyone who didn't want to be exactly who they were expected to be. Ginger was one of the Ever After High students who were a source of distress for him. "Professor Rumpelstiltskin gave me permission."

"Wish cakes can be very tricky." He ran his hand over his mustache and stared at her in a very serious way. "However, I am pleased that you're embracing your destiny. Potion-making is an important part of witchery. Proceed."

She didn't point out that her intentions were kind, rather than wicked, for fear he might change his mind. "Yes. Thank you."

Once she was inside the Cooking Class-ic Room, she began to prep for the show, measuring the dry ingredients into a bowl. The recipe yielded a thimble-sized cake, so the tiny measurements needed to be precise. Her hands trembled slightly, but she managed to do it perfectly. She placed a humming-bird egg on the counter, along with a pat of butter, to bring both to room temperature. Next came the most important part—the magic potion.

Ginger could bake a cake in her sleep, but a wish

potion came only once in a lifetime. It felt as if her entire future were riding on one recipe. She'd never been so stressed!

She'd decided that since she wasn't supposed to share the magic recipe with anyone else, she'd make it ahead of time. One by one, Ginger placed the potion's ingredients into a beaker. Then, using a pair of tongs, she held the beaker over dragon flame. The potion began to bubble. But the recipe didn't say how long it would take for the liquid to evaporate into a single drop. Her timing had to be perfect. A second too long and evaporation would be a hundred percent. A second too soon and she'd have two drops instead of one. This was where her experience would pay off. She waited. Intuition alone would determine her success. She noticed the fluid's motion and watched the steam emerge. *Wait for it*, she told herself, the tongs pinched in her fingers. *Wait. It's not ready yet. Wait.* And then, when she sensed it was the exact right time, she expertly removed the beaker from the flame. Once the steam had cleared, she peered inside.

All that was left was a single drop.

Ginger smiled. She'd done it! Then she glanced at the clock. It was almost time.

Humphrey and the Tech Club arrived with their bags of gear. Hopper was with them. He'd dressed a bit fancier than usual, adding a velvet bow tie that matched his embroidered jacket. And his hair was parted down the middle and slicked into place with some sort of oily hair product. "You look nice," Ginger told him.

"Uh...I do?" A small speck of color appeared on his cheeks.

Was he blushing? But he never blushed around her. Had he heard that she liked him? This was so embarrassing. "Whatever Faybelle told you, it's not true. It's—" His blush grew deeper. "Oh gosh, don't do that." If he turned into a frog, his wish might be entirely different. She opened the door to the pantry and pushed him inside. "Don't come out until I call you. I don't want you to talk to any girls until the cake is ready. I need you to stay in human form."

"Yeah, okay."

"Whoa!" Humphrey cried. He'd climbed onto a ladder to check one of the spotlights. His arms flailed as the ladder wobbled from side to side. "I could use some help over here!" Ginger closed the pantry door, then rushed to Humphrey's side.

"Please don't fall on your crown. Not today of all days."

"You're cracking me up," he said with a laugh. "Get it? *Cracking* me up."

Ginger was in no mood for jokes. She held the ladder steady until Humphrey climbed down. That was when Blondie popped her head into the room. "I've spread the word far and wide," she announced. "And I think you're going to be hextastic!" Then she threw open the door and students burst in. Royals and Rebels, cheerhexers and jocks, musicians and geeks—they crammed into the Cooking Class-ic classroom until it was full. Melody pushed to the front of the crowd.

Ginger couldn't believe her eyes. This was the kind of live audience she'd always wanted.

"Hopper, Hopper, Hopper!" students began to chant.

Okay, so maybe they hadn't come to see *her*, exactly, but it was still her cooking that would entertain them.

Daring and Sparrow entered. They squeezed to the front of the crowd. "Party!" Sparrow sang, striking his guitar.

Daring waved to the crowd. "Let the hexcitement commence," he said in a kingly way.

"Hey, *I'm* the director," Humphrey told him. "And no other cameras are allowed." He hustled Daring's camera crew out the door.

Blondie hurried around the counter and stood next to Ginger. "Well, at least that means the girls who would normally be watching *Daring's Day* will be watching your show, just to get a glimpse of Daring." She pointed to her MirrorPad. "I'll keep an eye on the numbers."

"Thanks. How do I look?" Ginger asked.

Blondie straightened the cupcake hat and wiped a bit of flour from Ginger's cheek. "You look great. Can you feel the anticipation? It's like the air is electrified."

The only thing Ginger could feel was her heart pounding against her rib cage. Humphrey stepped in front of the counter and raised his skinny arms. "Quiet on the set!" he hollered. After three more attempts, the audience settled down.

"Break a leg," Blondie whispered. Then she squeezed in next to Daring.

"It's not too hot in there, is it?" Ginger asked, peeking into the pantry.

"No," Hopper replied. He fiddled with his bow tie. "But is Briar out there?"

"Don't even *think* about Briar," Ginger told him. Then she closed the door. She didn't have the heart to tell him that Briar hadn't shown up. Briar was nicer than a good night's sleep, so it would be strange of her to miss the show, especially since Hopper's wish was based on her.

"Lights! Camera! Action!" Humphrey cried. The theme music swelled. Ginger tried to smile, but she was so nervous her face felt frozen. The theme music faded.

"Welcome to *Spells Kitchen*," she said. "Where good food is the secret ingredient to happiness."

Things didn't quite go as planned. She dropped a spatula on the floor. She knocked over a spice rack. Blondie kept constant vigil on the numbers, encouraging her now and then with a thumbs-up. With so many bodies in the room, the temperature rose. Sweat dotted Ginger's forehead as she mixed the batter. People kept whispering things like, "How long's this gonna take?" and "Where's Hopper?"

She poured the batter into a minimuffin pan and set it over dragon flame. It took only four seconds for the tiny cake to bake. "It's time to add the potion

containing the wishing spell." Ginger tipped the beaker. The single drop landed on the cake. Everyone said, "Oooh."

Ginger felt a bit better. This was going to be great.

"And now for the moment you've all been waiting for." A drumroll sounded from Melody's MirrorPhone. *Nice touch*, Ginger thought. Sparrow strummed some chords, which wasn't a nice touch. Everyone plugged their ears.

Ginger opened the closet door. "It's time," she said. Hopper stepped out. Whispered commentary arose from the girls in the audience.

"Will he actually be able to *talk* to us?"

"Without turning into a frog?"

"I don't think this will work."

"Yeah, no magic is strong enough to change Hopper. He's the prince of slimy pickup lines."

"More like the *king*."

"This is a waste of time. He'll never change."

Hopper frowned. His shoulders slumped. He suddenly looked as if he might flee from the room.

Ginger turned her back to the audience and spoke only to Hopper. "Hopper, don't listen to them. You can be whoever you want to be. Are you ready to make your wish?"

He shrugged. "Uh...I guess so."

When Ginger faced forward, Blondie gave her another thumbs-up. She set the little cake on a china plate, then held it up. Everyone went silent again. "The entire wish cake must be eaten," she instructed. "Then the wish must be spoken out loud." She took a deep breath and offered the cake to Hopper.

Silence descended. Except for Blondie, who shouted, "The number of viewers just tripled!"

Hopper grabbed the cake and shoved it into his mouth. "It tastes kinda weird," he said after swallowing. He coughed, then stuck out his tongue. "Ack! Really weird."

"I bet she poisoned him," someone whispered. "Just like her mother."

Ginger ignored the comment. The cake wasn't supposed to be delicious. It was supposed to be magical. She nodded at Hopper. "Go on, make your wish."

"I wish...uh...I wish...uh..." He paused. Ginger's heart skipped a beat. Had he forgotten his wish? "I wish to be able to talk to girls without turning into a frog." And then, as if she'd been waiting for her cue, Briar sauntered in.

"Am I late?" she asked.

Everyone turned and stared at her. Including Hopper. You could have heard a pin drop.

"Hi, Hopper," she said with a little wave. Then she whipped off her crownglasses. "I heard you want to talk to me without turning into a frog."

"Uh, hi," he mumbled. A faint pink color appeared in his cheeks. The blush was usually a sign that he was about to transform. But there was nothing to worry about. Ginger folded her arms and watched confidently as the blush spread down to his neck. It was working. The wish was working!

Poof.

The students laughed as Hopper the frog fell

through the air and landed behind the counter. Ginger stared down at him. "Uh-oh" was all she could manage to say.

Hopper the frog leaped onto a stool, then onto the counter. He stood on his back legs and addressed the audience. "Greetings, fair gentlemen and lovely ladies," he said in his booming baritone voice. "It is a conundrum to me that you find my froggy self so unappealing. Do you not admire my well-shaped legs and broad chest?"

As he puffed out his throat, some of the girls said, "Gross."

"Then you must admire my razor-sharp intellect and poetic dexterity." He began to strut up and down the counter, hands clasped behind his back. "Why should I wish to talk to girls without turning into a frog, when clearly I possess superior oratory skills when in frog form? Therefore, what I should have wished was to remain a frog forever after."

Some students groaned, some laughed. "Epic fail," Sparrow sang.

Ginger grabbed the recipe parchment. This wasn't happening. Had she missed a step? Had she forgotten an ingredient? "I need to take a nap," Briar said with a yawn. As she headed out the door, the other students followed.

Daring reached out and patted Hopper's green shoulder. "Good try, Hopper. See you back at the dorm." Then he strode from the classroom.

"Wait!" Ginger called. "I did it correctly. I know I did. I'll make it work. Come back!"

"Tough break," Blondie said as the room emptied. "The numbers are dwindling by the nanosecond. Down to sixty viewers, twenty viewers, seven viewers. Oh dear, now there are only two."

"That's a wrap!" Humphrey called. The Tech Club turned off the cameras and spotlights and began collecting the gear. "Sorry it didn't work out," he said. "Hey, Ginger, maybe you'd like to join the Tech Club and help us with other student Mirror-Casts?"

Ginger groaned, then angrily waved the recipe. "I

followed the directions," she insisted. "Why did he turn into a frog?"

Hopper the frog sat on all fours, a big frown spread from earhole to earhole. "Alas, it would thus appear that I have failed, once again, to enchant the fair beauty that is Briar." He hopped off the counter and out the door.

"You didn't fail!" Ginger called after him. "It's *my* fault. I did something wrong." But she didn't run after him. She turned away so no one could see the tears that stung the corners of her eyes.

Spells Kitchen was no more.

*T*he night passed so slowly Ginger began to wonder if Father Time was playing some kind of trick on her.

Melody told Ginger she was sorry things hadn't gone well. She gave Ginger a hug and drifted into such a deep, peaceful slumber she could have been mistaken for Sleeping Beauty's daughter. Ginger, on the other hand, lay on her quilt, staring at the wall, where the poster of her favorite spellebrity chef stared back at her. Not-So-Little Jack Horner was

known far and wide for his scrumptious pies and tarts. How many times had she imagined herself attending his prestigious cooking school? Or wearing a chef's hat just like his?

Was the demise of *Spells Kitchen* a sign that her dream wasn't meant to be?

Dawn trickled in through the window. Without a wink of sleep, Ginger was in a mood as dark as the circles under her eyes. She scrambled off the bed, stomped over to the wall, and pulled the poster from its tacks.

"You sure you want to do that?" Melody asked as she sat up in bed. "He's your idol, right?" Jelly stuck his head out of the water and nodded.

"Every time I look at this poster, it will remind me that I'll never be good enough to follow in his footsteps," Ginger said. She shoved the poster into her closet.

"It's not my place to judge," Melody said as she grabbed her headphones, "but I think you might be overreacting."

"Overreacting?" Ginger cried. "What if you told everyone that you were going to DJ a party and no one showed up? Or what if *everyone* showed up but you couldn't get the music to work, and your reputation was ruined?"

Melody nodded. "Yeah, okay. I get it. Yesterday was horrid for you. But you still have friends. And you still make the best treats at Ever After High."

At that moment, having friends and being a great pastry chef didn't feel like enough to Ginger. Yesterday's failure stung, not only because it had embarrassed her, but also because it had embarrassed Hopper. That old familiar feeling of not wanting to be noticed came flooding back. So, instead of her usual candy-colored clothes and frosted tights, she found a pair of plain leggings and a plain T-shirt. And instead of her favorite cupcake hat, she pulled an Ever After High cap over her pink hair, tugging the rim down low to hide her eyes.

"Who *are* you?" Blondie asked as Ginger stepped

into the hallway. "And what have you done with Ginger?"

"I don't want to talk about it," Ginger grumbled, slinging her cauldron purse over her shoulder.

"You can't hide anything from me," Blondie said with a gentle pat. "I'll get you to talk about it. I always do."

As they headed toward the Castleteria for breakfast, it appeared that everyone else was going about their day as usual. The end of *Spells Kitchen* hadn't changed anyone's life. Only Ginger's.

Faybelle flew past, then did a sharp 180-degree turn and landed right in front of Ginger, her arms crossed. "You look terrible," she told her.

"What do you want?" Ginger asked.

"Just so you know, I'm still angry that you didn't choose me to be on your show, even though your recipe was a spelltacular failure."

Ginger glared at the future Dark Fairy. "I'm not scared of you, Faybelle. Do whatever you want. I'm already in a rotten mood. You can't make it any worse!"

"Oooh, I sense a scoop," Blondie said, pulling her MirrorPad from her book bag. At first, Ginger thought Blondie was going to record the argument, but something else had caught the reporter's roving eye. She hurried down the hall, where Daring, still dressed in his pajamas, was looking at himself in a mirror. A cluster of sighing girls stood around him.

"Hi, Daring," Blondie said, elbowing a couple of girls until they made room. "Is something going on?"

"Turn off the camera," he told her, holding his hand in front of her MirrorPad's lens. "I'm in no mood to be filmed today. I didn't get a wink of sleep. And now I have…" He leaned closer to the mirror. "I have dark circles under my eyes!" He said this as if the world had come to an end.

Blondie shrugged. "I don't see any dark circles. You look as perfect as ever."

"Well, of course they are *perfect* dark circles, but they are dark circles nonetheless," Daring boasted. "This is Hopper's fault. He croaked all night long. What am I going to do? Makeup!" Three of the girls pulled powder puffs from their pockets.

Ginger didn't care about Daring's beauty crisis. A powder puff couldn't fix her life.

"Hopper croaked and croaked," Daring explained as the girls fought to dab makeup under his eyes. "He refused to turn back into a prince. How can I be expected to get my eight hours of beauty sleep with *ribbit, ribbit, ribbit* coming from the other side of the room?"

Ribbit, ribbit? Ginger paused. She'd never heard Hopper the frog make actual frog noises. He usually recited poetry.

With all eyes on Daring, Ginger slipped away. She headed back toward the dormitory. Something was very wrong, and it had nothing to do with Daring's face. Hopper always turned back into a boy. He usually retained his frog form for only a

matter of minutes. His curse, to be a frog forever until a princess kissed him, was not supposed to happen until he was an adult. That was how most of the curses worked. Like Duchess Swan turning into a swan forever, and Briar Beauty falling into a slumber of one hundred years.

So why was Hopper still a frog?

Frog Forever
After

wo family crests were mounted on the door, one for Charming, the other for Croakington. Ginger knocked. No one answered. "Hopper?" she said. She knocked again, then looked around. The hallway was empty. Everyone had headed out for breakfast. "Hopper?" She pressed her ear to the door.

Ribbit, ribbit.

Ginger turned the knob and entered.

She'd never been in Hopper and Daring's room before. It smelled like gym socks and Daring's cologne. Since both boys came from wealthy families, no expense had been spared. Both beds were covered in opulent fabrics and fur pelts. Daring's side was exactly as she'd expected. There were dozens of portraits of him. His face was even printed on his pillow. His shelves were filled with trophies for things like dragon-slaying and damsel-rescuing. Athletic equipment lay everywhere—swords, balls, jousting lances. And so many mirrors! One was mounted above his desk.

Hopper's shelves were also filled with trophies, for Swim Team and the long jump. A couple of extra crowns sat on his desk, and his closet was full of embroidered jackets and loafers. The big difference was that Hopper hadn't plastered photos of himself all over his walls.

There was one photo, however. Taped next to his desk. Of Briar.

Ribbit, ribbit.

Hopper the frog sat on a pillow, a little crown perched on his head. A dragonfly flitted above him.

Ginger had seen the dragonfly only a few times before. He was Hopper's pet and his name was Drake. "Hi, Hopper," she said with a wave. "I knocked, but you didn't answer. I hope you don't mind that I let myself in."

He blinked in that weird way that frogs blink, with his eyeballs half disappearing into his head.

She stood awkwardly next to the bed. A soft breeze drifted in from the open window. "How are you?" He didn't reply. "Daring said you've been a frog all night. Is that true?"

With a stretch of his hind legs, he leaped onto the windowsill. Then his tongue shot out of his mouth and he captured a housefly that happened to be in the wrong place at the wrong time. He swallowed.

Ew. She'd never seen him eat a fly before.

"Hopper, are you mad at me because the wish cake didn't work?" No answer. Was he giving her the silent treatment? "I'm sorry about that." She sat on the edge of the bed and sighed. "I tried to help you get together with Briar. Really I did. But nothing worked out. You feel embarrassed again and I've lost my show."

Ribbit, ribbit.

Something very strange was going on. Hopper didn't stand on his hind legs, or wave his arms through the air, or bow as he usually did. He sat very frog-like, his little suction cup toes splayed on the windowsill. His neck pulsated as he softly croaked. "Are you staying in frog form on purpose? I didn't know you could do that. I didn't know you could talk like a frog, either."

Ginger suddenly felt light-headed as the truth dawned on her. She darted to her feet. "Oh my god-mother, I know what happened! Wishing to be able to talk to girls didn't work, because it's a big wish. And the wish cake only grants a small wish."

Maybe she should have felt some relief, realizing that she wasn't a *total* failure. She'd followed the recipe correctly, after all. Her skills as a chef were perfection. How could she have doubted herself?

Then she gasped. Slowly, she turned toward the

window. "But you made a second wish, didn't you?" She searched her memory for the words that Hopper the frog had spoken.

Therefore, what I should have wished was to remain a frog forever after.

A frog. He'd wished to be a frog.

That was definitely a *little* wish.

Holy croak!

As Ginger realized that she'd turned the boy she liked into a real frog, Hopper leaped from the sill and disappeared into the garden below. Drake the dragonfly flew after him.

Eenie

Meenie

"*H*opper!" Ginger cried as she pushed open the dormitory's front door and ran outside.

Ever After High was surrounded by beautifully manicured gardens, so everywhere she looked, she saw green. The grass grew as thick and luxurious as mermaid's hair. The hedgerows and shrubs were covered in dense green foliage. There were too many places for a frog to hide. "Hopper!"

A couple of students glanced at her.

She darted around a rosebush, her eyes searching

the grass. "Hopper," she whispered. If he'd turned into a real frog, would he be able to understand her? She scuttled around. "Hopper. Hopper." Where was he? He had no idea how to take care of himself in the wild.

"Whatever is going on?" Blondie had sneaked up on Ginger in her usual way. "I was interviewing Daring and you disappeared."

"I'm just, ya know, enjoying the sunshine." Ginger stepped back onto the walkway. She didn't want Blondie in the grass, where she might accidentally step on Hopper. It was bad enough that Hopper was a real frog; he didn't need to get squished, too.

Blondie smiled. "I'm going to edit my interview with Daring and upload it right away. I've never seen Daring not looking perfect. This scoop will get a zillion views." Her fingers flew over her screen.

Ginger caught a streak of green out of the corner of her eye, then a little splash sounded from the nearby swan pool. *Uh-oh.* Did swans eat frogs? Ginger ran to the edge of the pool. There he was, frog-kicking his way through the water, his little gold crown still on his head. "Hopper," she called. The swans looked up. One of them eyed him. Was that a look of hunger? "Don't eat him!" Ginger yelled. She didn't bother taking off her shoes. She climbed into the pool and waded as quickly as she could. Two swans hissed at her.

"What are you doing?" Blondie called.

Those little green legs were fast. When the Candy Witch went frog hunting, she'd take a sturdy net. And she'd chant a little song.

Eenie, meenie, miney, moe
Catch a froggy by its toe

Ginger didn't have a net and she certainly didn't feel like singing. She finally caught up to Hopper only because he'd stopped to eat a water bug. She scooped him into her hands. "Gotcha!"

"Ms. Breadhouse!" Headmaster Grimm stood at the side of the pool. "There is no swimming allowed in the swan pool." He pointed to a sign.

THERE IS NO SWIMMING ALLOWED IN THE SWAN POOL.

"Sorry," she called as she clasped Hopper in her hands. He sure was wiggly. Then she stepped out of the water and smiled politely at the headmaster.

"What are you doing, Ms. Breadhouse?" He looked down his long nose at her. Her leggings dripped. A lily pad was stuck to her shoe.

"Uh, I'm just..." One of Hopper's legs slipped out between her fingers. "I'm catching frogs."

The headmaster raised an eyebrow. "I see." Then he surprised Ginger with a smile. "That is good news, indeed. Your mother is a skilled frogger, is she not? I understand the legs make an excellent soup. If this is a sign that you are taking your witchy heritage seriously, then I am most pleased." With a sharp turn on his heels, he began to walk away.

"Don't worry, I'm not going to put you into a soup," Ginger whispered into her clasped hands. She opened one of her fingers so his little head could poke out. He was still wearing his crown.

"Now are you going to tell me what's going on?" Blondie asked. "Why are you holding on to Hopper?"

Ginger glanced around. A few students sat on benches, but they were chatting on their Mirror-Phones. No one seemed to be paying attention to her. "I've done something terrible," she told Blondie. "I've turned Hopper into a frog."

Blondie frowned. "I don't understand. Hopper always turns into a frog."

"But this time he's a *real* frog. He doesn't recite poetry. He croaks. He eats bugs!"

Ribbit, ribbit.

"The wish cake worked. Hopper wished to be a frog forever after. Now he is."

Blondie leaned in close, peering at the frog in Ginger's hands. "He does seem slimier, if that's possible. And he *is* making weird sounds. If what you say is true, this is going to be the biggest scoop

since the news about the dish breaking up with the spoon."

"Please don't say anything," Ginger pleaded. "I'm asking you as a friend. If word gets out that I turned him into a real frog—"

"How very interesting," a snarky voice said. Faybelle had glided over, her wings as silent as a breeze. Ginger gasped, then closed her fingers over Hopper's froggy head. "Oh, you can't hide your mess, Ginger Breadhouse. I heard everything."

"You're *really* good at sneaking up on people," Blondie said, looking impressed. "I should get a pair of wings."

Faybelle flew a slow circle around Ginger. "What will Hopper's parents say when they find out that you've turned their precious son into a real frog?"

"Don't tell his parents," Ginger said. "Don't tell anyone. I'm going to turn him back."

"How?"

Ginger had no idea.

Faybelle continued to circle. "I bet Headmaster Grimm will be happy to hear that you've embraced your destiny and poisoned one of your fellow students."

"Poisoned?" Ginger started to clench her hands into fists, but then she remembered she was holding Hopper captive.

Blondie shook a finger in Faybelle's face. "That's a rotten thing to say. Ginger didn't poison anyone. Hopper wished this on himself."

"I don't really care *how* it happened," Faybelle said. "I'm going to tell everyone that Ginger poisoned Hopper on purpose. And that she'll poison the rest of us if we let her."

"She's ruthless," Blondie said as Faybelle flew away.

"This is a disaster," Ginger said. "No one will ever trust my cooking again." Hopper wiggled in her hands. "I know, I know, it's a disaster for you, too," she told him. Then she sighed. "I've got to figure out how to turn him back into a boy."

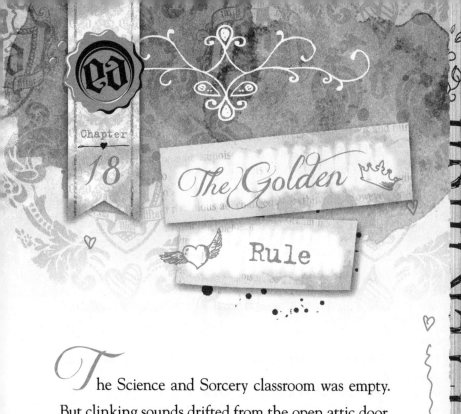

The Golden

Rule

The Science and Sorcery classroom was empty. But clinking sounds drifted from the open attic door. "Professor?" Ginger called. No answer. The clinking grew louder.

She couldn't climb the ladder and hold Hopper at the same time, so she opened her cauldron purse and tucked him into a pocket. He blinked at her. "Don't worry," she told him gently. "It'll be okay. I'm going to fix this." He didn't look concerned, or even interested. Maybe he couldn't understand a word she was saying.

The ladder wobbled and creaked as she climbed, rung over rung. Then she poked her head into the attic.

It was hot up there. A spinning wheel and a wooden stool sat in the corner, surrounded by piles of straw. The stool was empty. It appeared no one had failed a pop quiz and needed hextra credit that day, but it was still early. The clinking came from the opposite corner, where Rumpelstiltskin sat cross-legged on the floor, stacking a pile of gold coins. "Professor?"

He pushed his floppy hat from his eyes. "Vhadda ya vant?" Even when not teaching, he tended to shout. His booming voice filled the attic space.

She climbed off the last rung, then hurried toward her Science and Sorcery professor. "I need your help." Kneeling, so she wouldn't tower over him, she opened her purse and pulled out Hopper. A couple

of decorating sprinkles were stuck to his skin. She really needed to clean out that bag.

Rumpelstiltskin grunted. "Vhy bring me frog?"

Ginger realized that Hopper's crown had fallen off. She shuffled through her purse until she found it. Then she plopped it onto his head. "It's Hopper. I mean, it used to be Hopper. Or it still is Hopper. I'm not sure."

"You make no sense." He began a new stack of coins.

"I followed the recipe and made the wish cake. Hopper ate it just as planned. But he wished that he could talk to girls without turning into a frog, and it didn't work."

"Only little vish vork."

"Yes, that's what happened. He made a second wish. A little wish." She held Hopper up so Rumpelstiltskin could get a good look. "He wished to be a frog forever after. Now look at him."

Ribbit, ribbit.

"You made good vish cake. You get good grade. Now go!"

"I don't want a good grade. I want—"

"You no vant good grade?" He raised his bushy eyebrows. "You vant to fail? I give you bad grade. You spin gold for me." He pointed to the spinning wheel.

"No, no. I do want a good grade. But I don't want Hopper to be a frog forever after. I need to change him back."

"Vhy you vant to change him?" Rumpelstiltskin snorted. "You ever hear of rule of gold?"

"Rule of gold?" Ginger asked. "You mean the golden rule?"

"*Da*, that's it!" He pointed a hairy finger in the air. "You vant to be chef, not vitch. So you let Hopper be frog, not boy, since dat's vhat he vant. Leave him alone. Dat is golden rule."

That wasn't *exactly* the golden rule, but Ginger understood what the professor was trying to say. She wanted to choose her own path, so she should afford Hopper the same consideration. "But he doesn't want to be a frog. His wish was a mistake. He didn't mean it. He was embarrassed and upset. It's not really what he wants."

Rumpelstiltskin snorted. Then he kept counting.

"Professor? How do I reverse the spell?"

"No reverse. He made little vish. It's done!"

"But there has to be a way." Ginger looked down at Hopper's green face. "I know I can make only one wish cake, but what if someone else made a wish cake and the new wish was to turn Hopper back to normal?"

"To turn frog into boy is big vish, not little vish." He stacked the last coin, then scrambled to his feet. "Now leave me in peace. I get ready for date vith Candy Vitch. She bring picnic of homemade food just like Momma Rumpelstiltskin used to make. Maybe my beard vill explode again!" He did a little hop.

"The date's today?" Ginger said, somewhat startled.

That was when Hopper made his escape. He

soared from her hand and hopped across the attic floor. Quick as a wink, he leaped onto the ladder, then began making his way down the rungs. Ginger darted past her professor and scrambled down the ladder as fast as she could. But by the time her shoes touched the classroom floor, Hopper was already out the door.

"Breadcrumbs! Not again!" She ran outside. A hawk circled above the trees, scanning the ground for food. The swans glided in their pool, waiting patiently for a scrumptious morsel to swim in their direction. "Hopper, where are you?" Ginger called.

She caught something pink out of the corner of her eye. She whipped around.

A beautiful woman was walking up the lane toward the school.

A Nonpoisoned Picnic

Ginger did not feel embarrassed as her mother walked up the lane. And no one fled in terror. There was no pointed hat. There were no military boots. And not a single green hair to be seen. Ms. Bread-house wore a lime-sherbet pantsuit with matching heels. Her pink hair was silky and curled at the shoulders. A necklace of fruity loops completed the "normal" outfit.

"Hello, sweetie pie," she said, a picnic basket swinging from her hand. She'd touched up her roots

and pasted her false eyelashes in the right spots. A dab of makeup covered her chin wart. "Why are you dressed like that? Where's your cupcake hat?"

"Uh, hi, Mom." Ginger hugged her, then shuffled nervously in place. She didn't feel like explaining her wardrobe choices. Not while so much was at stake. She looked at the picnic basket. "You didn't happen to find a frog, did you?"

"It's been a long time since I collected eyeballs," Ms. Breadhouse said with an excited cackle. "Would you like to take a stroll this evening and do some frogging?"

"No!" Ginger said. "No frog hunting while you're here. Promise?"

Ms. Breadhouse sighed, her shoulders sinking. "Anything for you, my little Gingerpoo." She patted the basket. "I brought a lovely lunch for Rumpelstiltskin. I got all the recipes from a nonpoisonous cookbook, just to make you happy."

"Huh?" Ginger furrowed her brow.

"Well, I am trying to fit in. So I made cucumber

sandwiches with extra mayo." She reached into the basket, then gave Ginger a sandwich. "Go on, give it a try. You'll be so proud."

The sandwich was crustless and cut into a perfect triangle. Ginger peeled back the bread and was happy to discover no frog legs or spider legs. She took a bite.

"Well?" Ms. Breadhouse asked.

"It's good," Ginger said, which was a total lie. The sandwich tasted as bland as air.

"I've also made a gelatin salad with miniature marshmallows, and iced tea. It will be the most normal picnic ever." Ms. Breadhouse sighed again. She looked as unhappy as one of her poisoning victims. "And the most boring."

For as long as she could remember, Ginger had wanted her mother to make this kind of food. But now it just seemed so wrong. "Mom, you can't serve this."

"What do you mean?"

"Professor Rumpelstiltskin is expecting you to

poison him. He wants your witchy cooking. He wants his beard to explode. That's the kind of picnic I thought you'd bring."

"This is very confusing, my dearest. First you don't want me to poison people, and now you do." She set the picnic basket on the ground. "Do you want me to be Ms. Breadhouse or the Candy Witch?"

Ginger didn't want to hurt her mom's feelings. She was so grateful to her for agreeing to have lunch with Rumpelstiltskin. "I'm sorry, Mom, I know it's confusing. I'm very confused about a lot of things right now. I only promised Rumpelstiltskin a date with you because he gave me that special recipe, but now everything's a mess and he doesn't have another recipe to fix things. And I don't know who—"

Ginger gasped. Of course! She was standing face-to-face with an expert on recipes. Her mother was way more knowledgeable than Rumpelstiltskin. Surely she'd know how to change Hopper back into a boy.

If Ginger ever found him again.

"Mom, I need your help."

"Of course, my little lovey-dovey. What can I do?"

"Remember how I told you I was going to make a wish cake and feed it to my friend Hopper?" Ms. Breadhouse nodded. "Well, I turned him into a frog. A *real* frog."

"You turned the boy you like into a frog? That's nice, sweetie. I'm very proud of you."

"You don't understand." Ginger scooted her glasses up her nose and stared into her mother's swamp-green eyes. "I'm a total failure. Hopper doesn't really want to be a frog forever after. He was just saying that because he was embarrassed. I was trying to help him, and trying to help myself at the same time. But all I did was mess everything up."

The Candy Witch pointed a perfectly polished nail at her daughter. "You listen here, Ginger Bread-house. As much as it pains me to say this, you were put on this earth to create delicious, nonpoisonous treats. You were meant to decorate the world with icing swirls and chocolate sprinkles. *That* is your true destiny. And changing your clothing, or quitting your show, won't change who you are inside. Sharing your baking with others is what you do. It's your passion. You must always be true to yourself."

Changing your clothing won't change who you are inside.

Ginger looked at her mother's pantsuit. "Are you talking about me, or about you?"

"I guess I'm talking about both of us."

"Mom, you hate being Ms. Breadhouse, don't you?"

"I love being your mother, but I'm also the Candy Witch. Both of those roles are *my* destiny."

At that moment, Ginger saw her mother not as a character from a fairytale, and not as a parent, but as a person like herself. A person with talent and passion.

"Mom, I'm not a little kid anymore. And I'm at a school where everyone knows my story. I want you to go back to being yourself. I want you to be happy."

"Really?" She gasped. "But what about your

friends? Don't you worry what they might think about you?"

"I'm tired of worrying about what people think of me. My true friends accept me for who I am *and* where I come from." It felt so good to say those words, to have those feelings. Ginger laughed. Ms. Breadhouse cackled as if a giant weight had been lifted. Then they hugged.

"I'll change back into myself if you promise to do the same," she said, pointing to Ginger's bland clothing.

"It's a deal," Ginger said. "But right now I need to change Hopper back into himself. Do you have a recipe that can reverse wishes?"

"Let me think about this." Ms. Breadhouse narrowed her eyes. "This boy is the son of the Frog Prince, correct?"

"Yes."

She smiled. "Smoochy-poochy, there's only one way to turn a frog into a prince. And it doesn't require a recipe of any sort."

The answer hit Ginger so hard it almost toppled her over. "A kiss from a princess!" she cried. "That's the answer!" Now that she knew what to do, there was just one other tiny problem. "But how do I find him?"

"If he's turned into a *real* frog, then I'm guessing he'd go where most of the other frogs go—to the Ever After High swamp. When I was a student here, that's where I did all my best frogging."

"Thanks," Ginger said. She hugged her mom again.

Ms. Breadhouse picked up the picnic basket. "I'd better hurry home and pack a new lunch. If Rumpelstiltskin wants a date with the Candy Witch, he's going to want authentic Candy Witch treats." She smiled. "This will be so much fun!"

"Bye," Ginger called as her mother hurried back down the lane.

Ginger was so happy to have a solution she twirled in place. A princess kiss would reverse the spell.

It was Hopper's *only* chance, but at least he had a chance.

And fortunately for Hopper, princesses were as abundant at Ever After High as chips in a razzle-dazzle chip cookie.

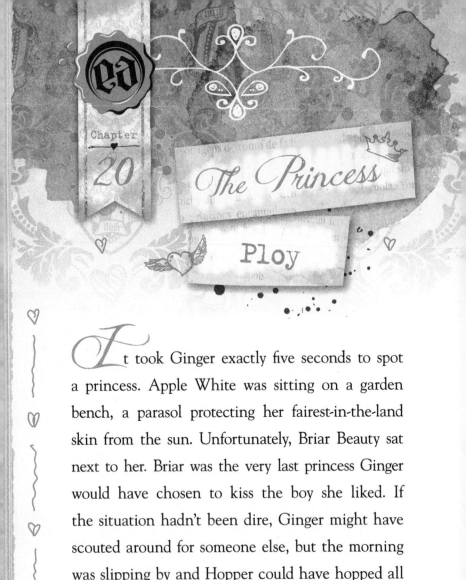

Chapter

20

The Princess

Ploy

It took Ginger exactly five seconds to spot a princess. Apple White was sitting on a garden bench, a parasol protecting her fairest-in-the-land skin from the sun. Unfortunately, Briar Beauty sat next to her. Briar was the very last princess Ginger would have chosen to kiss the boy she liked. If the situation hadn't been dire, Ginger might have scouted around for someone else, but the morning was slipping by and Hopper could have hopped all the way to Wonderland by now!

Thankfully, Briar was fast asleep. Maybe she wouldn't wake up.

"Hi," Ginger whispered as she quietly slid onto the bench.

"Hi, Ginger." Apple White smiled in her sweet, dimpled way. A pair of butterflies flitted around her head. She smelled like baby powder and apple blossoms. "I barely recognized you in that outfit. Are all your other clothes dirty? Do you need the number for my laundry dwarf?"

"No, I need to talk to you. I need a princess."

Apple turned and elbowed Briar. "Wake up. Ginger needs to talk to us."

"Oh, no, you don't have to wake her."

"Huh?" With a snort, Briar sat up straight. "Oh, hi, Ginger." She wiped a bit of drool from the corner of her mouth. "What's going on?"

Ginger's gaze darted between Apple and Briar. This was going to be impossible. If they wouldn't kiss Hopper in the kissing booth, they certainly wouldn't kiss him now. Would they? "I need your help with something. It's really important."

Briar yawned. "Faybelle told us that you poisoned Hopper and turned him into a real frog."

"That's not entirely true," Ginger said. "I—"

"Are you going to poison *us*?" Apple giggled and twirled her parasol. "I think it's lovely that you're following your wicked destiny. I tell Raven all the time that she can give me a poisoned apple, but she never does. It's so disappointing."

"I didn't poison Hopper. I made a wish cake and—" Why waste time defending herself? The girls were staring at her as if they didn't believe a word she was saying. "Never mind. What matters is that Hopper's been turned into a real frog, and he'll stay that way forever after unless we break the spell."

"We?" Briar asked. "But you're the one who poisoned him."

"I didn't...ugh! Look, do you know the story of the Frog Prince?"

Apple batted her long lashes. "Of course we know

that story, silly. We learn every royal story in Princess-ology class."

"Then you know that in order to turn Hopper back into a prince, a princess needs to kiss him."

"Kiss a *real* frog?" Briar asked. "Ew, ew, and more ew."

"I have to agree," Apple said with a pout. "That doesn't sound very appealing."

How could Ginger make her request *appealing*? She couldn't put frosting on it or dip it in Candy Mountain chocolate sauce. What appealed to princesses?

"Duty," she said, looking directly at Apple. "It's your *duty* to kiss him."

"Oh my goodness," Apple said. She clapped her hands. "You're so right, Ginger. It's a tough job, but if no one else will step forward, then yes, indeed, it is my duty."

Briar's eyebrows rose in surprise. "What in Ever After do you mean it's *your* duty?"

"Well, my story is the *most* well-known and the

most popular, so it makes sense that I'm the right one to turn a frog back into a prince." She smiled, but not in a snobby way. Apple believed everything she'd just said.

Briar chuckled. "Have you flipped your crown? Your story is far from the only princess story around. My kiss would work just as well as your kiss."

"I'm not so sure about that," Apple said matter-of-factly. "My fairytale is always on the bestseller list, and I hate to say this, Briar, but people often confuse you with that *other* beauty, the one who meets the beast."

"That's so not true!"

Were they actually arguing about who should kiss Hopper? Why couldn't they have shown this much enthusiasm when Hopper had been standing in the kissing booth? But that scene had happened and it couldn't be rewritten.

A hawk circled above their heads, its piercing gaze scanning the ground for prey. Ginger darted to her feet. She hated what she was about to say, but the

clock was ticking and frog-eating predators were hunting. "Look, you can *both* kiss him. Let's just go find him before it's too late."

Apple tried to get to her feet first, but Briar was quicker. "I'll find him!"

"No, I will!" Apple's little outburst scared the butterflies away. It was unlike Apple to get so snippy. But she took duty very seriously.

And then things took a turn in a direction Ginger would never have imagined. Two more princesses walked up to the bench—Ashlynn Ella and Raven Queen. "What are you arguing about?" Ashlynn asked.

"Hopper's waiting to be kissed and turned back into a prince," Apple said. "I'm the best princess for the job."

"Not in my storybook," Briar grumbled. "Clearly, *I'm* the best princess for the job. My kiss will break the spell."

Ashlynn pointed to herself. "Uh, hello? I'm a princess, too. My kiss is just as good as your kisses."

Ginger tried to get a few words in, but the princesses started arguing even louder. The noise drew stares from passing students. Raven cleared her throat, then raised her hands, which made everyone a little nervous because Raven was capable of conjuring magic. "Settle down, ladies." Though she didn't follow in her Evil Queen mother's footsteps, she could command attention when she wanted. The arguing ceased. "I'm no expert on kissing, but we have a friend who needs our help. It seems to me that we should be working together to save Hopper."

The princesses nodded in agreement.

"Thank you," Ginger said. "Now let's get to the swamp!"

Apple frowned. "Oh dear, no one said anything about a swamp."

The Ever After

Swamp

efore they set out for the swamp, there was a heated discussion among the princesses about the perils of traveling to such a dank, soggy place. They spritzed themselves with bug repellent and stuffed their pockets with antislime wipes. Since most of the princesses had sophisticated taste in shoes, they borrowed galoshes from the Hero Training class-room. And when Apple mentioned that she'd heard frogs can give you warts, they grabbed some wart remover from the nurse's office. Remembering all her frog-catching lessons, Ginger grabbed a couple of butterfly nets.

"Wait for me," Blondie cried. "I'm a princess, too."

"Well, actually..." Raven looked as if she was going to argue this point, but Apple poked her in the side. "Uh, right. Sure."

"One of my sources leaked your quest," Blondie explained. "Well, actually, I was eavesdropping. But that's why I'm the best reporter on campus. I want to capture all the action for my show." She pulled out her MirrorPad and pressed RECORD. Then she held it in front of her face. "Hello, fellow fairytales. Blondie Lockes here, recording from the gardens of Ever After High. The question I put to you is this: Is a princess's kiss powerful enough to turn a frog back into a prince, or is that another fable fed to us by our storybooks?"

"It's not a fable," Apple said. She smiled at the camera. "There is no kiss more powerful than a princess's kiss."

"That's not entirely true," Raven said. "True love's

kiss is the most powerful. We just learned that in Princessology."

"This is very interesting, but we need to start walking," Ginger said with a sense of urgency. She balanced the butterfly nets on her shoulder. "Everybody follow me."

It wasn't difficult to find the swamp. Headmaster Grimm insisted that the groundskeepers post signs all over campus so that no one would get lost. One sign led to the Village of Book End, another to the Enchanted Forest, another to Mirror Beach. "Here we are," Ginger said as they stood in front of a small green sign.

EVER AFTER HIGH SWAMP, THIS WAY ☞

WARNING: TREACHEROUS PATHS, CREEPY CRAWLIES, AND FOUL ODORS AWAIT THOSE WHO ENTER THIS REALM.

"Sounds like home," Raven said drily.

Ginger led the way down the dirt path. The going

was slow, thanks to roots and loose rocks. The forest grew thick in these parts, with ivy and brambles filling the spaces between trees. Moss hung from branches in long strips like Rapunzel's hair.

"Hopper!" Ginger called. "The last time I saw him he was still wearing his crown, so he should be easy to spot. Hopper!"

"Everybody be careful," Ashlynn advised. "There are lots of critters that crawl along the forest floor, and we wouldn't want to step on any of them."

"Yes, watch your step," Ginger said, trying not to imagine what a squished Hopper would look like. She was grateful that Ashlynn had decided to join them. The princess had a special relationship with nature. In fact, she could talk to many creatures.

Hoot!

"What was that?" Blondie asked a bit nervously.

"An owl," Ashlynn said. "He's complaining that we woke him from his nap."

"I'd like to take a nap," Briar said with a yawn. She sank onto a boulder.

"Now is not the time for beauty sleep," Apple said, pulling Briar to her feet.

"Hopper!" Ginger called again. "Hopper, don't worry. We're coming to help you!"

As they walked deeper into the forest, the air grew humid and the path became soggy. Their galoshes slurped through the mud. Water dripped from moss. Red toadstools with white polka dots appeared in clusters. The fattest toadstool had a little chimney sticking out the top and smoke coming out. "Maybe whoever lives there can help us?" Raven suggested. She bent over and, using one fingernail, tapped on the door. "Hello? Anyone home?"

The shutters opened and a tiny head popped out the window. "You be interrupting me teatime!" It was a smallfolk.

Ginger peered over Raven's shoulder. The scent of peppermint drifted from the tiny creature's teacup. She'd never met a smallfolk before. Maybe it could help them find Hopper. "Sorry to bother you,"

Ginger said. "But we're looking for the Frog Prince. Did you happen to see him hop this way?"

The smallfolk grumbled something to itself, then glared up at Ginger. "I be seeing a froggy with a crown hop past, if that's what you be asking about."

"Oh, that's great news," Ginger said.

"Which way did he go?" Raven asked.

"Where all froggies be going." The smallfolk leaned out the window and pointed down the path toward the swamp. "At least froggies be knowing their place. Unlike you bigfolk, always stomping about where you don't be belonging. Now leave me to be drinking me tea in peace. And watch where you be stepping with those big foots of yours." The little head disappeared into the toadstool, and the shutters slammed shut.

"What a grouch," Blondie said.

"Smallfolk don't like us much," Ashlynn explained. "They are the caretakers of the forest floor, and we're always messing things up."

"My feet are *not* big," Apple said with a *humph*.

Her hopes reignited, Ginger scrambled back onto

the path. Then she took her place in front and continued to lead the way. "Hopper, we haven't forgotten about you!"

Blondie picked a strand of moss from her golden curls. "This is *so* not right. Are we there yet?"

"Ick." Apple plugged her quaint little nose. "What's that smell?"

"Swamp gas," Ginger told her. Her childhood kitchen had often been filled with that stench while her mother brewed. "That means we're getting close."

"Listen," Ashlynn said. "I hear them." The distinct sound of croaking drifted down the path. "I haven't learned amphibian yet, but they do sound happy, don't you think?"

Raven shrugged. "They sound like frogs."

Then, just as Ginger was about to step over a gnarled root, something sparkly caught her eye. She reached down and picked up a tiny crown. "Look," she said, holding it up for the others to see. "He was definitely here."

Hoot!

Everyone looked up at the forest canopy. A pair of yellow eyes gazed down at them. "The owl says we're interrupting his hunting," Ashlynn whispered.

Raven narrowed her dark eyes. "Let's just hope the crown fell off Hopper's head by accident instead of being knocked off by a pair of talons."

Knocked off? "Don't eat my friend!" Ginger said, pointing up at the owl. "You hear me? Tell him, Ashlynn. Tell him not to eat Hopper."

Ashlynn hooted a couple of times, then shrugged. "My owlspeak is pretty rusty. I'm not sure if I said 'don't eat the Frog Prince' or 'don't eat before swimming.'" Either way, the owl didn't reply. He just blinked his full moon eyes.

If owls were hunting, then what else was hunting? Had Hopper already been eaten? Ginger picked up the pace and bumped right into a sign. "Here it is!" she cried.

WELCOME TO THE EVER AFTER HIGH SWAMP.
ENTER AT YOUR OWN RISK.

After pushing some branches aside, Ginger stepped over a log and around a clump of reeds and stood at the water's edge.

At first, it looked as if the murky swamp were filled with floating eyeballs, but then Ginger realized that the eyeballs belonged to swimming frogs. "There are way too many," Blondie said. "How will we find Hopper?"

"We'll just have to kiss them all," Ginger realized.

"Kiss them all?" Briar cringed. "Seriously?"

"That's going to take forever after," Ashlynn said.

Raven folded her arms. "Is it too late to change my mind and un-volunteer for this quest?"

Ginger's heart began to pound. After coming all this way, were they going to give up? "It won't be that bad," she said, trying to reassure the princesses. "There are only about fifty frogs in here. Well, maybe more like one hundred. Okay, possibly two hundred...or so. But that's not bad. We can do this."

"We?" Briar snorted. "*You* don't have to do the kissing, Ginger. You're not a princess."

"Lucky girl," Raven said.

Apple took a tube of charm gloss from her pocket. "Duty calls, ladies. No complaining. We are princesses, and turning a frog back into a prince is one of our most important obligations." She glossed her lips. Then she grabbed a net, stepped into the water, caught a frog, and kissed it. Just like that.

"Wait, I wasn't ready." Blondie fumbled with her MirrorPad. "Can you do that again? I want to get a close-up. My viewers are going to love this." She pressed RECORD and started shooting. But Apple had already released the first frog and had caught a new victim. *Smooch.* Then she grabbed another. *Smooch.* And another.

"Hey, she's trying to kiss them all herself. She wants to be the one to save Hopper." Briar slogged into the water and rolled up her sleeve. "You're not the only princess around here." She plunged her arm into the muck and pulled out a wiggling frog. Then she cringed, puckered up, and planted a kiss on the top of its head. "Ack," she said. "That was disgusting."

"Oh, don't hurt its feelings," Ashlynn told her as she stepped cautiously into the water. "And be careful, everyone. Step lightly so you don't hurt anything."

Ginger couldn't believe her eyes. The princesses were actually catching and kissing frogs. Though Ginger was smiling, the frogs didn't look too pleased. They'd been minding their own business, going about their day, and suddenly found themselves being plucked from the water and kissed by total strangers. They squirmed and kicked, then leaped to freedom as soon as the kiss was over. Unfortunately, not a single one turned into Hopper the boy.

As it turned out, Ginger's mother had taught her well—her frogging skills were undeniable. She quickly filled one of the nets with frogs and handed it to Raven, who was sitting on a log, rolling up her leggings. "All these are for me? How *thoughtful* of you."

"I'd help kiss, but I'm not a princess," Ginger said with an apologetic shrug. As she began to fill another net, she listened intently, in case one of the frogs decided to recite poetry or to declare his love for Briar. That would have made things super easy. But no frog spoke any word except for *croak* or *ribbit*.

Just as she reached for another frog, a dragonfly flitted in Ginger's face. She swatted at it. But it flew around her head, hovering near her ear. What an annoyance. "Go away," she grumbled. It circled two more times, then landed on a rock, right next to a frog. Either the dragonfly was clueless that frogs eat bugs or...

"Drake?" A shiver ran up Ginger's spine. The dragonfly nodded and blew a tiny flame from his mouth. Ginger almost shouted with joy. Drake the dragonfly was showing her Hopper.

"Can you tell my viewers how you're feeling?" Blondie asked, interviewing the princesses.

"My mouth tastes weird," Ashlynn complained.

"My lips are sticky," Apple said.

"Frog is definitely an acquired taste," Briar said, making a gagging sound.

Raven sighed. "No comment."

Ginger held her breath. The frog's eyes were closed. He didn't seem to know that Ginger was hovering over him. The poor little thing looked so tired after his long journey. Ginger didn't announce that she'd found Hopper. She didn't want to do anything that might startle him. Ever so slowly, with fingers extending, she reached out. The dragonfly watched, his wings vibrating in place. "Gotcha!"

"Oh, not another one," Raven said. "I'm not even done with this batch."

The frog's eyes popped open. He squirmed as Ginger lifted him until he was level with her face. "Hopper?" she whispered.

He kept squirming.

Then Ginger did something, even though there was no rational reason to do it. She wasn't a princess. But at that moment, she was overcome with instinct, pure and simple.

She kissed the top of the frog's head.

Happy Hopper

*W*hat happened? Where am I?"

Hopper the boy stood up to his knees in swamp water. Clumps of moss clung to his jacket and his hair was a bit messed up, but those adorable freckles were still in place. Drake the dragonfly flew around his head, then landed on his shoulder.

Hopper looked around, his expression tight with confusion. "Why...?" He gulped. "What...?" He scratched his head. "Where...?"

At first, Ginger didn't smile, because she felt

equally confused. "Don't be scared," she said. "It's a long story and—"

"There he is!" Briar exclaimed. She dropped a frog and sloshed through the water until she was standing next to Hopper.

All the princesses spun around. Upon seeing Hopper, they stopped kissing, dropped their frogs, and hurried over. Blondie climbed onto a tree trunk so she could get a better shot with her MirrorPad.

"Welcome back," Raven said to Hopper.

"I did it." Briar beamed proudly. "I broke the spell."

"I'm royally sorry to say this, Briar, but what makes you think it was you?" Apple asked. "It could have been my kiss."

"Or mine," Ashlynn said.

"Would somebody please tell me why I'm standing in this..." Hopper looked at the water. "Swamp?"

"I kissed you," Briar informed him. "And you're welcome." Then she took an antislime wipe from her bag and cleaned her crownglasses. "My work here is done. Let's go, girls, or we'll be late for afternoon classes."

"And there you have it, my fellow fairytales." Blondie was talking into her microphone. "Briar Beauty has broken the spell with her princess kiss, and Hopper Croakington is, once again, a boy."

Apple frowned. "I still think it was my kiss." She smiled at Hopper. "Surely you remember who kissed you."

"Kissed me?" Hopper loosened his bow tie. "I don't remember being kissed."

"Ginger was the only girl standing on this side of the swamp," Ashlynn pointed out. "Maybe she saw something. Ginger, did you see Hopper swim over here after being kissed? And did you see who kissed him?"

Ginger knew exactly who had kissed Hopper, and it hadn't been a princess. But that could mean only one thing. Her head was spinning. "I didn't see anything," she lied.

"Then we'll never know who broke the spell," Raven said. "So there's no use arguing about it."

They quickly emptied water from their galoshes and cleaned slime off their hands. Then the princesses started back down the path. "Wait," Blondie called. "I want to get some postquest interviews." MirrorPad in hand, she hurried after them.

Ginger and Hopper were still standing in the swamp, looking equally dazed.

"Let me get this straight," Hopper said. "Briar... *kissed* me? She really kissed me?"

Ginger weighed the consequences of telling the truth. If she admitted to the boy she liked that it had been *her* kiss that had saved his life, she'd be the hero. Hopper would be very grateful; he might even change his feelings toward her. He might even start to *like* her. But she'd also be admitting that a true love's kiss had saved him. And that was way more than she wanted to admit. She liked Hopper—that was certain—but *true love*? Besides, he seemed so happy with the notion that Briar had saved him. She wanted him to be happy, after all, and she was glad to have her friend back. Maybe it just wasn't the right time to tell him the truth.

"Uh...yeah, it was Briar. You needed a princess kiss to turn you back." And then she told him the whole story, about how he'd wished to be a frog, how he'd turned into one, and how everyone had joined together to find him.

"Whoa. All I remember is that I was on your show, I went back to my room, and the rest is blank." Then he beamed. "I can't believe they came out here to kiss me." He looked as if he were going to burst from happiness. "Briar kissed me."

The moment was truly bittersweet. "We'd better get back." Ginger waded from the swamp, sat on a log, and emptied her galoshes.

As they started down the path, Drake flew up ahead, leading the way. There was a happy rhythm to Hopper's steps. On Friday morning he'd stood in the kissing booth, completely ignored. Now he knew that several of the fairest princesses at Ever After High had tried to kiss him. Had *wanted* to kiss him.

Ginger sighed. She was happy to have Hopper back, happy to see him smiling, and happy he didn't know the truth. She just wasn't ready for true love. Not yet.

As she wiped frog slime off her hands, she giggled to herself. Someday she'd kiss Hopper the boy. And that day was worth waiting for.

Chef

Ginger

*H*umphrey looked at his watch. "Fifteen minutes until showtime," he said. "Are you sure your special guest is coming?"

"Yes, I'm sure." Ginger was back to her old self. She'd chosen a lemon-yellow dress with peppermint buttons, frosted tights, and a pair of icing-dipped shoes. A chef's hat shaped like a towering birthday cake sat atop her head.

A couple of days had passed since the frog-kissing expedition. Blondie had made the story the highlight of her show. She'd replayed the footage a dozen times, and for days and days, it was what everyone talked about. And it got far more viewers than *Daring's Day*. Luckily, Blondie hadn't recorded the actual kiss, so Ginger's leading role in breaking the spell remained a secret.

Hopper got a lot of attention that week. He even created some new pickup lines based on his experience. "Wanna hop over to my place?" "Only your kiss can break my spell." "It's no croak—I'm hoppy to see you."

Even Daring was impressed. "Way to go, roomie," he'd said with a high five. "The princesses were lining up to kiss you. Are you sure you're not related to a Charming?"

As Ginger cleaned the counter and Humphrey checked the lights, Hopper took his place behind Camera 2. "Thanks for talking the tech crew into giving me another chance," Ginger said to him.

"No problem," Hopper said. "I wouldn't be here if you hadn't helped me."

You've no idea, she thought with a smile.

Blondie entered the classroom, followed by a long line of students. "You'll have no problem getting viewers," she happily told Ginger. "Now that everyone knows your wish cake was a success, they want to know what's next." She hugged Ginger. "I'm so proud of you. We're going to have the most watched shows at Ever After High. It's our destiny."

Melody waved. So did Briar, Apple, and Ashlynn. "Can't wait to see what you cook today," Cedar Wood said. The room quickly filled. Even Faybelle flew in. She glared at Ginger but didn't say anything.

"Ten minutes to showtime," Humphrey announced.

Then everyone turned and gasped as a woman in a tall black hat strode into the room. "Gingerpoo, Mommy's here."

Ginger didn't cringe. She didn't try to hide. Instead, she waved.

The audience parted, leaving a path for the Candy Witch. Her green hair was matted with twigs and brambles. Her ratty old black dress was patched with burlap, and her military boots were caked with mud. A wiry black hair had sprouted from her chin wart.

Blondie elbowed Ginger. "Uh, what's *she* doing here?"

Ginger stepped in front of the counter and raised her hands to get the audience's attention. "Everyone, this is my mother, the Candy Witch, and she's going to be my guest today on *Spells Kitchen*."

At first, no one said a word. Ginger waited, her stomach tightening. Would they jeer? Or leave? The Candy Witch had such a wicked reputation—how would Ginger's friends react? Then Blondie broke the silence. "Brilliant!" she said as she wrapped an arm around Ginger's shoulder. "You'll get a zillion viewers. Now you're thinking like a true spellebrity chef."

As the tech crew made final adjustments and the audience chatted, the Candy Witch set a picnic basket on the counter. "Rumpelstiltskin and I rescheduled our date for after your show," she told Ginger. "Look what I brought. This'll be a date he'll never forget." She opened the basket to reveal a loaf of bread that was wiggling. "Worm loaf," she said. Then she pointed to a wedge of cheese. "I poisoned the cheese with a brand-new recipe. It makes holes in the cheese *and* holes in the eater." She cackled. "It's just temporary, of course. No guts will fall out." Then she held up a bottle. "We'll finish the meal with this lovely brew."

"Did you poison it?"

"Of course. One sip and Rumpelstiltskin's toes will sprout teeth!" The picnic basket shuddered, then emitted a loud belch.

"That's great, Mom. He'll love it." Ginger quickly closed the basket so the odor wouldn't invade the room. Then she set the basket aside. "But remember, today we're going to cook something *non*poisonous."

"Of course, sweetie. This is your show, after all. I'm so proud of you."

There were a few minutes until showtime, so Ginger went around the room and introduced each of her friends to her mother. And when her mother offered them a piece of candy, they each politely declined. Faybelle shook her hand. "It's so nice to see you again, Ms. Candy Witch. My mom is always telling me how good you are at wicked witchery. Did you hear, Ginger and I are lab partners in Science and Sorcery?" She put her arm on Ginger's shoulder as if they were the dearest of friends. "We daughters of villains should stick together, don't you think? I'm trying to persuade her to follow in your bootsteps."

The Candy Witch cackled. "There's no need to do that. She's got a mind of her own, and I like it that way."

Faybelle frowned.

"I just sent a hext to the entire student body that your mom's the guest," Blondie said. "Your viewer numbers will soar."

"Places, everyone," Humphrey called. Ginger took her mom's hand and led her behind the counter.

She didn't bother handing her mother a pink apron. The days of trying to pretend that her mother was someone else were over. And Ginger wasn't going to pretend to be someone else, either.

Ginger Breadhouse, daughter of the Candy Witch, had been cooking long enough to know that the reason her mother's cucumber sandwich had been flavorless was that it had been prepared without joy. Food made without joy wasn't nourishing. A life without joy wasn't nourishing, either.

"Ready?" she asked her mom.

"Ready," her mom said with a black-toothed smile.

"Lights! Camera! Action!" Theme music swelled.

"Hello, everyone. I'm Ginger Breadhouse. Welcome to *Spells Kitchen*, where good food is the secret ingredient to happiness."

Acknowledgments

It was fun writing this book because, well, I hate to admit it, but I'm a terrible cook. My mother, however, is incredible. She makes everything from scratch. We grew up with homemade sourdough bread, her famous angel food cake, and homemade tortillas. When Ginger talks about good food bringing happiness, I thought of my mom's cooking.

The world of Ever After High is an enormous, ever-changing place, filled with more details than one person can remember all by herself, so I lean on a cast of writers, editors, and designers to help keep track of everything. I am so grateful to the team

at Mattel and the team at Little, Brown Books for
Young Readers. They are, in no particular order:
Pam Garfinkel, Erin Stein, Mary-Kate Gaudet,
Christine Ma, Rachel Poloski, Nicole Corse, Robert
Rudman, Audu Paden, and Julia Phelps.

And a very special thanks to Shannon Hale, for
leading the way.

About the Author

Suzanne Selfors feels like a Royal on some days and a Rebel on others. She's written many books for kids, including the Smells Like Dog series and the Imaginary Veterinary series.

She has two charming children and lives in a magical island kingdom, where she hopes it is her destiny to write stories forever after.

Ever After High™

CHOOSE YOUR OWN EVER AFTER™

Discover the World of Ever After High™

WATCH ON NETFLIX

Ginger Breadhouse™
DAUGHTER OF THE CANDY WITCH

Blondie Lockes™
DAUGHTER OF GOLDILOCKS

Check your local retailer for enchanting dolls and products!

 EVERAFTERHIGH.COM
Play games, watch videos and meet the spellbinding students.

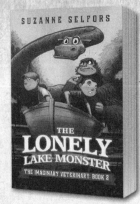

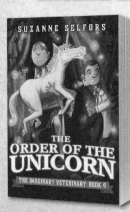
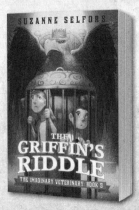